Billy
the
FISH

Billy the FISH

Charlie James

BLOOMSBURY

NEW YORK BERLIN LONDON

Text copyright © 2006 by C. Wilson
Illustrations copyright © 2006 by Ned Jolliffe

All rights reserved. No part of this book may be used or reproduced
in any manner whatsoever without written permission from the publisher,
except in the case of brief quotations embodied in critical articles or reviews.

Published by Bloomsbury Publishing, New York, London, and Berlin

Library of Congress Cataloging-in-Publication Data
James, Charlie.
Billy the Fish / by Charlie James ; illustrations by Ned Jolliffe.
p.   cm.
Summary: After eating Dad's experimental fish food,
Ned's little brother turns into a cod and finds himself sharing
an aquarium tank with Kylie the killer whale.
ISBN-10: 1-58234-732-8 • ISBN-13: 978-1-58234-732-5 (hardcover)
ISBN-10: 1-58234-733-6 • ISBN-13: 978-1-58234-733-2 (paperback)
[1. Brothers—Fiction. 2. Fishes—Fiction. 3. Humorous stories.]
I. Jolliffe, Ned, ill. II. Title.
PZ7.J153597Bi 2006   [Fic]—dc22   2006042663

First U.S. Edition 2006
Typeset by Dorchester Typesetting Group Ltd.
Printed in the U.S.A. by Quebecor World Fairfield
4 6 8 10 9 7 5 3

Bloomsbury Publishing, Children's Books, U.S.A.
175 Fifth Avenue, New York, NY 10010

All papers used by Bloomsbury Publishing are natural, recyclable products
made from wood grown in well-managed forests. The manufacturing processes
conform to the environmental regulations of the country of origin.

For Mark, Charlotte, and James

Contents

PROLOGUE

I hate fish.

They are slippery. They are scaly. And, let's face it, they stink.

So when my brother turned into a cod, I was, quite frankly, disgusted.

I mean, a *cod*? Have you seen what they look like? They are ugly and flabby and they taste like cardboard—especially when served under a thick white sauce with green specks. Mom calls it "parsley sauce." I call it "seaweed sludge."

I ask you, if he was going to turn into a fish, couldn't the idiot have turned into something slightly more exciting?

Couldn't he at least have been—well, a *shark*?

Chapter 1

BILL IS BORED

I blame Bill.

I think it was all his fault. Of course, he doesn't agree with me. He swears it was all an accident and that he didn't mean to do anything wrong.

Didn't mean to do anything wrong? Well, excuse me for breathing, but who does he think he is? I mean, can we just take a quick reality check?

Here's a list.

THINGS I HAD TO DO FOR BILL (BUT REALLY WISH I HADN'T)

1. Rescue him from the jaws of death, not once—but twice.

2. Face the local bully.
3. Risk total and utter social humiliation in front of the whole school.

You see? And all because of the things Bill did that he shouldn't have done. Get the picture? That boy is nuts.

Bill is my younger brother. He is six years old and has blond hair, blue eyes, and a tendency for lice. Those who don't know him think he looks like an angel—but if Bill's an angel, heaven has a problem. It's not that Bill is nasty or anything like that. It's just that, well, Bill is Trouble—Trouble with a capital T. Whatever he does, wherever he goes, Trouble follows, particularly when Bill is bored. And on this particular day, Bill was *particularly* bored . . .

It was Saturday. Dad was out, Mom was in the garden, and Stacey (my sister) was in her bedroom painting her nails a disgusting shade of blue. As for me, I was lying in bed pretending to be ill. Now, before you think I'm completely pathetic, there was a reason—though it is really embarrassing, and I can hardly bring myself to write the truth. You see, I was—*ahem*—cramming for the Interschool

Quiz Championship, and I didn't want anyone—least of all my parents—to know.

Let me try to explain . . .

The Interschool Quiz Championship is held once every three years. It is a huge event, and schools from all around the town compete to win the mega first prize. And this year it was immense—a brand, spanking new entertainment system complete with the latest PlayStation, wide-screen TV, and surround-sound cinema. Sound good? You bet! Look good? Even better!

There was only one tiny little problem with my plan—me. I can never remember a single fact, no matter hard I try—unlike my younger brother, who was born with the best memory I've ever come across. I read all the books and look at all the information. But looking is as far as it goes. It's in one eye and out the other. As soon as anyone asks me anything, I start to panic. My face turns red, my palms start to sweat, and I look like a halibut on toast (or so Stacey kindly tells me). It's totally gross. But by then, I was too desperate to care. I was ready to risk everything to win that prize.

And if you're wondering why I didn't ask my

parents for help—well, the answer's simple: it's because of PDS (Parental Disapproval Syndrome). They simply don't approve of PlayStations or TVs or computers or anything that's at all necessary or important in life. Forget about entertainment; all they want us to do is eat our five portions of fruit and veggies and play outside. Honestly, it's so unfair. I'm sure it's against our human rights or something. Just to prove my point, here are the (completely idiotic) reasons why I believe we are the only family on the block not to have a PlayStation, let alone any gadgets that don't predate the bubonic plague:

Dad: "A PlayStation is not a fish."

I know, I know. This is a difficult one to get your head around, but if you can just bear with me for a few more pages, I'll try and explain.

Mom: "A PlayStation is not organic, educational, powered by fresh air, or attached to a ball of wool."

Mom is crazy about knitting.

Stacey: "A PlayStation is not a boy/makeup/hair gel/an item of clothing/a cell phone accessory, etc., etc."

Welcome to Planet Stacey.

And wow, are our parents stubborn. Bill and I have tried and tried to change their minds at least a hundred zillion times. We even offered to make our beds in the morning (well, once a week at least). But each time they spit out the same tired excuses:

Mom (to Bill): "Whaddya-need-a-PlayStation-for-when-you-could-play-outside-in-the-fresh-air-instead-of-being-cooped-up-inside-all-day-staring-at-a-screen?"

It was Christmas.
It was snowing.
I rest my case.

Dad (to me): "In my-day-boys-had-to-amuse-themselves-and-make-their-own-toys, chairs, tables, beds . . . !" Oops! Slight exaggeration there. Sorry, it just slipped in . . . Back to Dad.

"And-anyway-don't-you-think-you-should-be-studying-math-and-have-you-done-your-homework-yet?"

See what I mean? I don't think he understands the concept of free time.

As for Stacey . . . Well, I am sure she would help us if she could get her brain into gear. She used to be really fun, but all she does now is read magazines and sigh—a lot! Bill thinks her brain's gone soft from washing her hair twice a day, but I think girls are just *weird*.

Anyway—back to boring Saturday and why my brother was in such a bad mood. Bill was bored because Mom and Dad were busy, Stacey wouldn't give him the time of day, and I . . . well, I was lying in a darkened room with a towel wrapped around my head, like a total nutjob, trying to study. And the worst of it was, I couldn't tell anyone my plan. My parents would have lectured me about how I was doing it for the wrong reasons (you know the kind of thing):

Dad: "Education is an end in itself!"
Mom: "You shouldn't need bribes to work hard!"

Even if I *did* win, I bet they'd have made me promise to give the stuff away so that they could replace it with an educational toy. Stacey wasn't interested, and try as I might, I could not bring myself to tell Bill. Even if he could keep his mouth shut, it would raise his hopes, and he would only get disappointed if I failed. So, no, I had to do it alone. This was my secret.

Little did I know then that there was another secret-keeper in our family.

Which brings me neatly back to Saturday and Bill.

Chapter 2
BILL'S SECRET

Bill tried very hard to get me out of bed that morning. He knew I was faking it and longed to know what was going on. But I just lay there groaning artistically and begging him—in a faint voice—not to open the curtains, as the light hurt my eyes. It was an Oscar-winning performance, if I do say so myself.

When it was very clear that I wasn't going to budge, he got into a bad mood and stomped downstairs into the kitchen, looking for something to eat. Bill is permanently hungry. Unfortunately for him, since Mom's gone on her latest health kick she's gotten rid of all the chips, cookies, and chocolate bars and replaced them with dried fruit and carrot juice.

But, being Bill, he was in luck. At the back of a cupboard that took him a mere five minutes to ransack, he found the last bag of his favorite Monster Munch chips—the ones in a bright purple bag with a picture of a pterodactyl being devoured by a Tyrannosaurus rex. Bill loves chips, and this flavor—pickle and tomato—was his favorite. They were history in a matter of nanoseconds.

After that, his luck ran out.

Despite an intensive search, Bill found nothing else worth eating. But he did notice a large and important-looking box on the kitchen table. It was addressed to Dad. On the top and on each side were large labels with red lettering.

To be fair to Bill, it was lying around for anyone to see.

But, to be fair to us, anyone else in our family would have read the warning and left it alone.

Bill, though, is different. Bill, if you remember, was bored. Trouble was on its way.

He read the warning labels on the box. (Bill is seriously smart and can read almost as well as I can.) He immediately went into "curious mode" and decided to explore some more.

Bill opened the box.

It was full of multicolored bags labeled "FISH CHIPS." Inside, there was also a letter addressed to Dad. It wasn't in an envelope, so Bill decided it would be okay to read it. This is what it said:

Dear Mr. Finn:
Thank you for your box of Fish Chips for Homes and Aquariums. We think it is the best fish food in the world!

Please send us enough to feed our killer whale—the one we have just rescued from a film set in Hollywood. She arrives at the zoo next week, along with our new Marine Life Manager, Ms. Donna Mezzweme.

Yours sincerely,
Eimer Boss
Director
Z.E.B.R.A. (Zoos for Endangered Beasts and Rare Animals)

P.S. When we were testing your second set of samples—Super-Strong Fish Chips for Scarce Sea Fish—an expert here swears he saw a fish change shape briefly. Is this possible? Please do some more tests. The leftover bags are in this box. Annoyingly, their labels have become smudged with seawater.

P.P.S. Watch out! Guard your samples with care! We hear that those crafty crooks, The Underwater Underworld, are out to sabotage your valuable work to restock the oceans with fish. Their spies are everywhere! Do not let your Super-Strong Fish Chips for Scarce Sea Fish fall into the wrong hands. The future of the marine world depends on you, Mr. Finn!

Bill read the letter twice. Some of the words were new to him, but he made sense of them the second time around. He blinked. *Hollywood? Fish changing shape? Spies?* What on earth was going on?—and, more importantly, what was Dad up to? Until now, he'd always thought that Dad's fish food business was pretty dull and boring. All that stuff about increased haddock velocity and falling herring densities made his eyes water. How could it suddenly be so exciting? Surely it was up to him to find out. He decided there and then to help Dad survive in this murky underwater world—oh, and perhaps eat a few Fish Chips on the way. After all, anything had to be better than dried fruit. So he quickly stuffed as many bags of Fish Chips as he thought he could get away with into the pockets of his cargo pants, replaced the letter, and carefully closed the box.

Then he sat down to work out what to do next.

And no one was even the teensiest, weeniest bit suspicious about what he had done.

Except for me.

FISH SAMPLES!
IMPORTANT!
TOP SECRET!
WARNING! For fish only!
DEFINITELY NOT FOR HUMAN CONSUMPTION!

It was lunchtime, and upstairs in my bedroom, I was as hungry as Bill and twice as bored. I had been cramming for *three hours* (well, two and a half if you count that short recreational break I took to reach the next level on Bill's Game Boy—a present from sympathetic Glam Gran). But it was no good. I couldn't remember a single thing. There was nothing for me to do but to stage the fastest recovery the world has ever seen. I limped down to the kitchen to see what everyone was up to.

The first person I saw was Bill, who was lurking by the kitchen table, peering at a large box. He scowled at me—which I probably deserved—but I could tell he was up to something as soon as I saw his face. He was wearing that sort of shifty, I'm-up-to-no-good-and-I'm-not-going-to-let-on-what-it-is expression that I know only too well.

Just then, Mom bustled in from the garden and gave me a big hug. She was thrilled at my miraculous recovery and promised to make me a nice pot of boiled cod and tofu to keep my strength up. Personally, I would have preferred a fried egg and hash browns, but I could have eaten a table leg by that point. I nodded weakly and sat down next to Stacey, who had just appeared with the latest edition of her favorite magazine. She sniffed as though I was a pile of dog poop and looked away with a sigh.

Soon after that, Dad waltzed into the kitchen, waving a large carrier bag in the air.

He tapped the box on the table, then tapped his nose as he surveyed his family with a beaming smile.

"Ah, yes," he said happily, and almost to himself. "I was expecting this delivery."

There was a slight pause, and I noticed Bill watching Dad very closely. Dad, catching his eye, gave a quick start and seemed to pull himself together.

"Hello, Plankton! Hello, Sardines!" he said excitedly. "Have I got something to show you! Just wait 'til you cod-a-load of what I have here. You'll be thrilled!" And he banged his bag down on the mysterious box.

We all sighed—well, all of us except Mom. Dad can do no wrong in her eyes. She thinks he's great. So do we, for that matter, but it's just that sometimes, Dad is so . . . *Dad*. You see, he's an inventor—a fish food manufacturer who is obsessed with fish: breeding them, feeding them, cooking them, and eating them. It's his whole life, and the only thing—apart from us and Mom—that he's really interested in. Normally, I try to take an interest—it is his job, after all. But I had a gut feeling as I looked at this "TOP SECRET!" box that this was going to be one *plaice* too far.

Mom, sweet as ever, clapped her hands with excitement. "Oh, Dan!" she breathed. "Is it more news about your fish food samples?"

"Yup!" said Dad. "It is good, good news. This is it. I've finally done it. I've just invented the best fish food ever. Fish food that will get us noticed. Fish food that will make us rich! Fish food that will make—"

"Um, Dad?" I asked, interrupting him in mid-flow. If he went on uninterrupted, I might lose the will to live. "Just tell us why it's so good."

Dad coughed and looked a little furtive. Then, to our amazement, he started to behave in the oddest way—even for him. He scuttled around the room, checking behind doors and peering out of the window. Then he drew the curtains, turned on the kitchen faucet, and switched the radio on full blast.

Even Mom was puzzled. "Dan?" she asked. "What are you doing?"

"Ssh!" answered Dad, putting his finger to his lips. "Walls have ears!" And then, turning off the light, he took a flashlight out of his coat pocket, beckoned us around the kitchen table, and opened the box. The letter and the samples were still there. I noticed that Bill was standing very still, but even so, he seemed to rustle slightly if he moved. I looked at him suspiciously, but it was no good. Dad was holding the flashlight awkwardly and Bill's face was in shadow.

Then Dad cleared his throat importantly. "Right, Small Fries! Gather around and I'll tell you exactly what is going on."

Chapter 4
DAD'S SECRET

We all peered into the box. It was difficult to see much by flashlight. It was even more difficult to know what to say to Dad. I mean, the box didn't seem very special. In fact, it seemed full of perfectly ordinary bags of fish food called "Fish Chips." But Dad was gazing at them as if they were the crown jewels.

"Um, Dad," I said eventually, "what *exactly* are we supposed to be looking *at*?"

"These," said Dad, picking up a handful of bags and raising them up into the air, "are the Holy Grail of fish food."

"The Holy . . . what?" screeched Stacey, trying to make herself heard above the noise of the radio.

But Dad stood like a man transfixed. "The Holy Grail of fish food!" he said again. "Look at these bags. Together they contain the finest ingredients, guaranteed to make fish fitter, healthier, bigger, and better than ever before. Why, with these Fish Chips, we will be able to satisfy the hunger of any fish, from minnows to whales, whether they live in the smallest fish tank or the biggest sea. With my new patented fish food, we will restock the oceans, replenish the lakes, re—"

By a strange coincidence, this rousing speech was accompanied by some loud sweeping orchestral music on the radio. It was all too much.

"Stop! Stop, Dad!" I begged, looking at his glowing cheeks and shining eyes. "I'm sure they're really, really good. Truly I am. But why all this *fuss*?" I waved my hand around the room, pointing at the drawn curtains, the running water and the blaring radio.

Dad's eyes widened, and he turned bright red. "Because of *them*!" he muttered darkly.

"W-w-what do you mean, *'Them'*?" Mom asked nervously. Dad leaned forward so that we had to bend toward him to hear. And when we did, I must say I didn't believe him.

"Fish farmers!" Dad whispered triumphantly.

"*Fish farmers?*" repeated Mom. "*Fish farmers?* Surely *fish farmers* can't do us any harm?"

"Huh!" said Dad, rocking backward importantly on his heels. "That's what you might think, but how do you *know*? Those rascals would go to any lengths to get their hands on my fish food. There they are, busily farming their fish all over the world because the seas are running out of them. Then along I come with my bags of Super-Strong Fish Chips. One or two rounds of the stuff in the sea and—poof! Down goes their business. And up go

Finn's Fine Fish Foods' profits! The seas are full of fish; the fishing boats are full of fish; the shops are full of fish. Everyone is happy . . . or everyone," he lowered his voice again to a fierce whisper, "except the fish farmers and our fiercest fish food competitors." There was a dramatic pause. "Ah, well . . ." he added, cheering up and putting the chips back into the box, "I suppose it's technological breakthroughs like this that make my job so worthwhile."

He clicked off the flashlight and went to open the curtains, turn off the faucets, and switch off the music. I stared at him. I didn't get it. I mean, why bother? If the fish stocks in the seas are really that low, why don't we just stop eating fish? I certainly wouldn't object. I can't stand the stuff. But it didn't seem like the right time to mention this. And anyway, Stacey had a question.

"But, Dad, how are you going to make any money if you simply throw your fish food into the sea?"

"Ah, well, we're not—or at least not for a long time," said Dad, a little confusingly. "You see, we at Finn's Fine Fish Foods are developing two sorts of Fish Chips: one that will be sold to the public for use at home, as well as to large zoos and aquariums;

and a second type," he paused and tapped the box, "like this, which is being developed with government aid to help restock the seas. I call them the Super-Strong Fish Chips for Scarce Sea Fish. This kind of fish food will be much, much stronger than the others. That's why this box here needs to be kept hidden somewhere safe, somewhere that fish farmers and their sort will never think to look." He stopped talking and suddenly turned toward me. "Somewhere like Ned's wardrobe."

"Ned's wardrobe?" whispered Mom. "But it stinks, and you can't get anywhere near it. His clothes are all over the floor in front of it!" Her voice was faint. Like me, she was probably reeling from the thought of a pack of angry fish farmers, wearing yellow galoshes and wielding fish hooks, rampaging through my dirty underwear.

"Exactly!" said Dad triumphantly. "No one in their right mind would ever think of hiding such a valuable piece of research material there. Yes, this aquatic gold mine will be safe in Ned's wardrobe."

Which is absolutely and exactly where it was not.

Chapter 5
CHANGING
ROOMS

Have you ever had one of those dreams where everything goes wrong? I haven't, but I've heard of them, and if they are anything like what happened that afternoon, I don't ever want to risk sleeping again.

As soon as Dad closed the box, we all trooped upstairs to put it into my wardrobe—in my room. (Well, obviously it was my room because that's where I sleep—or slept. Things move quickly in my family.)

And that's when the "Finn family upheaval" began.

First of all, Bill was furious—even more furious than he had been that morning. As soon as I opened

the door, everybody saw what Mom calls "the mess" and I just call "general living." (You know the type of thing: clothes on the floor, shoes on the chairs, comics stuffed into the garbage . . . nothing out of the ordinary.) But Bill immediately spotted my books. And his Game Boy. On the bed. Where I'd been studying while pretending to be ill. He went crazy. Mental. Ballistic. On a chart of one to ten, he was at about nine trillion zillion. You see, it's one thing to be ignored by your older brother because he is—or at least claims to be—ill. It's quite another to be ignored because he is cramming for a test. That stinks. That sucks. As far as Bill was concerned, I was a nerd and a geek, and he was going to do three things. He would:

1. **Never speak to me again for the rest of his entire life, and he means that seriously. So there.**

2. Ask for his Super Mario Intergalactic Game Boy game back, instantly, and if it's broken, demand that it's replaced, with interest, out of my allowance.
3. Ask Mom if he can have my room, because if all I'm going to do in it is lie in bed and read books, then I might as well take a camp bed down to the local library and live there.

But Mom wasn't listening. She was worrying: worrying that a load of burglars in yellow galoshes would come into my room in the dead of night and trip over my dirty socks in order to steal Dad's box; worrying that I might get hurt; worrying that I was sleeping alone.

"But, Ned, Dan, this is *terrible*," she said, clutching at my sleeve and surveying the scene.

Well, I must admit, it was bad.

"Really, really *awful*."

I blinked and looked again. Well, I suppose it was wrong of me to have stuffed Action Man head first into a glass of dirty water, but I didn't think it was actually putting the family at risk.

And then Dad, trying to help, made it all a hundred times worse.

"Oh, no, dear! This room's perfect! Don't worry!" he said, patting her comfortingly on the shoulder. He lifted the box and tried, unsuccessfully, to pick his way through the mess on the floor to the door of the wardrobe. Something went crunch under his foot. It was Bill's Super Mario Intergalactic game for his Game Boy. I was dead. Utterly, totally caput.

Dad, of course, was as oblivious as ever. "There's no problem," he repeated reassuringly. "All Ned needs to do is keep everything just the way it is. D'you hear that, Ned? No—and I mean absolutely *no*—cleaning up!" And then he added the punch line, the one that will live in our household for the rest of time. "But of course, Ned's such a sensible boy, I know he can be relied on!"

"Sensible?" Stacey's banshee wail could be heard halfway down the street. "How can you even think that? Ned's nothing but a loser, a geek . . . a . . . a total zero! *I'm* the reliable one! *I'm* the one who's always having to fix things for them at school!" (What has Stacey ever fixed besides her hair?)

Because Mom seemed to be in a trance, it was up

to Dad to calm Stacey down. "N-n-now hold on—" he stuttered. But he was too late. Stacey was in a state—a martyr with a mission—off to orbit Planet Stacey in a stellar-sized tantrum. We had no choice but to listen quietly and hope that it wouldn't last any longer than usual.

But unfortunately for us, it did.

On and on she went. On and on and on. And on.

And, as ever, her tantrum followed the same well-worn pattern.

Tantrum One: *It's so unfair.*

"It's so unfair!" she shouted, waving her hands around at my crud-infested room. "Just because I'm the only girl in this house—" (Mom, being over thirty, clearly doesn't count) "—I get the short end of the stick. I mean—what *is* everyone complaining about? At least the stuff on my floor isn't a health hazard. My room is way, way neater than this . . . this . . . *pigpen!*" (I resent this insult! I mean, let's face it: if my room is a pigpen, hers is a municipal dump!)

She broke off, struck by a sudden thought. Casting aside her handkerchief (well, actually, it was one of my T-shirts, but I think we'll ignore that point), she looked up with a nasty glint in her eye that I know only too well. Tantrum Two was about to begin.

Tantrum Two: *How come he has more than me?*

"Hang on a moment," she cried accusingly, assessing the room as if for the first time. "How come Ned's got the biggest room anyway? He always has more than me! This should be my room! *I'm* the oldest! It's me who is the firstborn Finn! I deserve respect! *I'm* the biggest child—so *I* should have the biggest room. *And by the way, Ned,*" she hissed, stabbing her finger in the air at me, "before you say *anything,* when I say *big*—**I DON'T MEAN FAT!**"

Dad, eager to smooth things over, tried to interrupt a second time. But he shouldn't have bothered. Stamping her foot and behaving just like a heroine from a tacky TV soap opera, Stacey prepared to let rip her two all-time favorite themes:

Tantrum Three:
1) *Why do the boys always get more than me?*
2) *Why do you love them more than me?*

"I know why Ned's got this room! It's because he's a *boy*, isn't it? They always get what they want!" (NOT true! Don't forget the nonexistent PlayStation!) "I never get anything!" (Um, except for a lifetime's supply of superstrength, hard-as-nails hair spray.) "It's so unfaaiiiir! You've always preferred the boys to me!" (Actually, if anything, I think Dad prefers fish on the basis that they do not talk back!)

And with that, she took a deep breath and tossed her red mane of hair defiantly over her shoulder— a sure sign that we were about to start the grand slam (otherwise known as the "final Finn flounce").

"Well, as far as I'm concerned, I've had it!" she screamed. "Ned might be a nerdy little Goody Two-shoes, but what about me? I mean, hello! Excuse me, but this is the twenty-first century! Hasn't anyone in this family heard about women's rights?" Then, before any of us had time to reply, she continued, "No! Of course not! But that's oh-so-typical of the way this family operates! I mean, does anyone ever consider me? No. Do they ever wonder about my needs? No. Do they listen? Can I ever get a word in edgewise?" (Hello???!!!) "Of course not! No one understands me! No one loves me. Everyone hates me! I'm all a-a-lone . . . I can't take any mo-o-o-re . . ." she sobbed. But just as she was about to flounce out of the door (slamming it so hard that the windows rattled and the handle fell off), Mom came out of her trance and took the wind right out of her sails.

"Well, yes," she said, briskly. "Stacey's right!"

Stacey blinked, stopping mid-tantrum. No one said anything—mainly because our mouths were hanging open in shock.

Mom, ignoring the silence, continued on briskly. "Stacey can have this room . . . Ned can move into the top bunk bed in Billy's room." Bill stamped his foot in fury, but realized from the look on Mom's face that she was not in the mood to discuss it. "And then we can turn Stacey's old room into a study for Ned—look at the books all over the bed; he's obviously trying to study, bless him. I know it's going to be tough on Billy, but we'll try and make it up to him somehow . . . " Then, noticing that we were still unconvinced, she started to falter. "Well, maybe you'll enjoy sharing your room after all this time," she added lamely. "After all, hah hah," she tittered nervously, catching sight of Bill's tight-lipped jaw, "it might be nice for you to spend some quality time with your brother . . . "

She looked beseechingly at Bill, but he was not having it. He just wanted time to plunge me up to my neck in a vat of boiling oil. The truth was etched all over his face. Not only did he *not* get my old room, he didn't get Stacey's either—and that was twice as big as his. Instead, all he had ended up with was me, my dirty underwear, and loads of unwanted junk. There was no escaping the facts.

I had moved in one fell swoop from being the Most Disliked Person in the Room to being Mr. Evil, Public Enemy Number One.

But just as it seemed there was no hope for me, Dad fired off a second bombshell. For once in his life, he disagreed with Mom.

"No, Plankton," he said in a firm voice, ignoring Stacey's outraged squeal. "This is not going to work."

Well, of course it wasn't. I could have told him that. Nothing ever works in this house.

"Stacey cannot live with Ned's wardrobe in her room," Dad continued.

"Why not?" I protested. Until five minutes ago, I had spent my entire life in the company of that wardrobe.

"Stacey is a girl," said Dad, stating the obvious. "Say what she might about female rights, she might be in danger here on her own."

"Oh, Dad, you're so thoughtful," said Stacey, reaching up and kissing him on the cheek. "I'd be *so* worried if I thought those horrid fish farmers were going to sneak into the room and scare me half to death." To be honest, I couldn't disagree more. One snarl from her, and I think they'd be back to their lakes in an instant. They wouldn't stand a chance against her cutting comments and bright blue talons.

But Stacey hadn't finished. Aware that she had an audience, she snuggled up to Dad. "And I would," she added, looking around the room, "find it difficult to keep the room as messy as this, however hard I tried. You see, I'm naturally an organized person." And here she looked daggers at me. Ouch, does my sister know how to twist that knife. Do you think it's something that girls learn in kindergarten?

That clinched it. Stacey was given the big room— *my* bedroom, and the wardrobe—*my* wardrobe— was moved to Bill's—now *our*—bedroom.

Of course, it didn't fit. So we had to change the beds around so that they were crammed against one wall directly facing the wardrobe. This meant it was very awkward to get in and out of the bunks. By now, Bill was definitely not talking to anyone— which is always a bad sign. Anyhow, with a lot of huffing and puffing, we managed to squeeze the wardrobe in, open the door just far enough, and wedge the box of Fish Chips inside. But it wasn't something I would want to do more than once.

No, I figured that Dad, this time, was right. Any burglar aiming to steal the box from *this* room would find he had his work cut out for him.

We were safe.

We could relax.

We could, perhaps, even have lunch. I was starving. Even boiled cod and "seaweed sludge" sounded delicious by now.

But lunch was off the menu. Mom had a mission: to make the rest of the house presentable enough to be frisked by even the fussiest fish farmer. This left Dad to prepare lunch (never a smart move) and Stacey and I to argue over who should be the one to pick the pink chewing gum off of my old bedpost.

So it wasn't until later that we realized that Bill was missing.

Chapter 6 BILL GOES MISSING

Things weren't going well.

A whole hour had passed since we'd moved rooms, and we were still in total chaos. Dad's burnt lunch had set off the smoke alarm, and it was now beeping like crazy, making the dog bark nonstop. Mom kept yelling down the stairs for one of us to shut the kitchen door and wave a dish towel at the alarm, but if Dad heard her, he certainly hadn't understood. The high-pitched din was now threatening to out-squeal even Stacey's squawks.

As for the mess in my former room . . . well, I was fairly embarrassed, now that I looked at it—a motley assortment of clothes, sneakers, books, half-eaten candies, scrunched-up wrappers, and abandoned toys. I took some comfort from Stacey's ex-bedroom floor, which was littered with makeup and magazines. Bill's was scattered with broken catapults, pebbles, bits of wood, the jawbone he'd found on the porch, a hammer Dad had lost almost a year ago, and some unfinished Lego models. When I tried to suggest to Mom that mine wasn't bad in comparison, she silently pointed to Glam Gran's missing check book (reported stolen), the missing keys to a car we sold three years ago, a Tupperware box containing a festering cheese sandwich that she had made for my school trip last month, and worst of all, the first sweater she ever knitted me in hideous, rainbow-colored stripes. My claim that the dog must have eaten it had led to our poor mutt being banished to her doghouse for a week.

Mom was clearly so hurt and angry that she could hardly speak. She simply turned around and hissed for me to go *immediately* and tell my brother to come back *this minute* to help. I took one look at her face and made a quick exit. But I couldn't resist drawing her attention to Stacey's newly created sign for "her" bedroom door.

The new Queen of Clean had written:

Dear Fish Farmers
Dad's Super-Strong
Fish CHips for
Scarce Sea Fish
ARE NEXT DOOR
(in Ned's WARDROBE)
← Love
Stacey x

The arrow pointed directly toward Bill's room.

Stacey refused to take it down. Soon she and Mom were at each other's throats. She also refused to have anything to do with my mess. "I'm not touching one single smelly sock!" she yelled. "They're so stinky. I mean, what does Ned *do* with his stuff? Sniff this . . . " and, to prove her point, she grabbed one of my old sneakers and tried to shove it up Mom's nose.

Luckily, Stacey's new cell phone started to ring, saving us from any more abuse. It was her best friend, irritating Izzy. The phone glued to her left ear, Stacey forgot all about cleaning up her room and started moaning on about Mom and Dad and me and Bill, my books, my pathetic attempts at studying, my need for a brain as well as a study room, the unfairness of life/family/friends . . . oh yes, and the color of their friend Tracey's new hair extensions and which film star looked best at the Oscars. That cell phone—one ring and she is back on Planet Stacey in her own parallel universe.

Mom finally flipped. Yanking the phone out of Stacey's hand, she pushed her in the direction of a teetering pile of old magazines and bellowed (well, it was the only tone of voice Mom had left at that point) for Bill. But no one came. Bill had vanished.

Normally, Bill going missing would put everyone on red alert as it could only mean one of two things:

1. Bill was busy getting into trouble.
2. Bill had gotten into trouble and now trouble was busy waiting to get into him.

But things were not normal—not normal at all.

I looked everywhere I could think of in the house without success, so I decided to search the backyard. I tried the bushes . . . the tree house . . . the garden shed . . . but I couldn't find him anywhere. Bill had vanished.

I love our backyard. It is one of the best things about our house. It's huge and overgrown and a great place to play. When Glam Gran lived here, the yard was full of flowers and the lawn was always mowed. But now that she has given the house to us and spends her time shopping and sightseeing abroad, the whole place has been left to grow wild. Everywhere, that is, except for the ornamental pond.

The pond, which is at the bottom of the yard and out of sight of the house, is Dad's pride and joy. It has a large stone fountain and is completely weed-free. It's there that Dad keeps all his prize fish, including Goldie the Goldfish—he knows them all by name. It's one of Dad's favorite places. Bill likes it, too, which is why I thought he might be there.

I crept cautiously toward the pond, hoping to surprise my brother. I don't really like water—which perhaps explains why I don't really like fish. Water makes me nervous, especially when it's anywhere near Bill. It gives him a chance to get up to—or get into—trouble. But there was no one there. Instead, floating on the surface of the pool, were two empty bags of Dad's new patented Fish Chips.

My heart started to thump. I felt an icy chill run up and down my spine. How could the bags have gotten there? Dad was in the kitchen, making (or *trying* to make) lunch. Mom and Stacey were locked in the mother of all bedroom battles. So who else could have possibly found these bags of Fish Chips? No one—unless . . . I froze, gripped by a terrible thought. Unless, perhaps, they had already been stolen by a fish farmer! And if some fish farmers had managed to get their hands on Dad's fish food, could they have managed to get their hands on Bill, too? I picked up a large stick and tried to be brave. I felt a bit idiotic, but I didn't know who was lurking in the trees around me.

There was a sudden movement in the water, followed by splashing and gurgling noises. My heart leapt. "Bill!" I shouted, edging toward the pond. I peered into the water, still clutching my stick. All I could see was Goldie the

50

oversized goldfish, slowly swimming backward and forward.

Then something caught my eye. Just behind Goldie there was a large, ugly fish that I had never seen before: a huge cod, with what looked like a single golden curl coming out of the top of its head. I swear it looked familiar. Too surprised to be frightened, I crouched down onto my hands and knees to take a closer look.

"B-Bill?" I faltered.

THWACK! No sooner had I muttered his name, than the ugly cod jumped out of the water and smacked me hard across the forehead, leaving a nasty, smelly smear of fish scales in my hair.

"OWWW!" I yelled at the top of my lungs, falling backward. "You stupid, stupid fish, what on earth did you do that for? That hurt!" I glared at the pool, but the fish had disappeared.

"Dumb fish!" I shouted out to no one in particular. "If there are any fish farmers here, they are welcome to any bags of Dad's fish food they can find!" I stomped back into the house in an absolute fit. Bill or no Bill, I wanted my lunch, and at that point, I did not want to go near any kind of pond or hear the word "fish" ever again.

Chapter 7

THE MIS-TAKE

When I got back to the house, Dad had set the toaster on fire for the second time, and once we had doused the flames, everyone had forgotten about Bill. It probably had something to do with the hunger pangs. I had even (temporarily) forgotten about the two mysteriously empty bags of Dad's fish food floating on the pond—and being slapped in the face by a cod. All I could think about was lunch—or the lack of it. Dad had given up; Stacey was in a huff and, with the air of a martyr, said she couldn't possibly make lunch because she was too busy cleaning up her room *alone*; and Mom was knitting.

This is always a bad sign. Mom's a worrier by nature, and when she's worried, she knits. She collects odd bits of leftover organically dyed wool that she turns into strange sweaters and socks that she expects us to wear. Looking at her white face and trembling hands, I figured we were in for a flock of virulent orange tank tops.

I sighed. This was an emergency. I picked up the phone. I speed-dialed the local pizza delivery shop, and within ten minutes, we were sitting down to a feast of tomato and mozzarella double-thick pizzas, garlic bread, and dough balls. All except Mom, who said that she'd have an organic bean salad once she'd completed a particularly intricate part of her knitting pattern. As soon as the pizza boxes were opened, Bill appeared. Honestly, my brother can smell a chocolate bar being unwrapped from fifty feet away. Pizza is his second favorite food. It's amazing.

What was also amazing was that:

1. Bill was in a really good mood.
2. He was slightly damp and there was a long, straggly bit of green seaweed hanging over his left ear.

Mom looked at him suspiciously, put down her knitting, and felt his clothes.

"Billy, what have you been up to?" she asked.

Bill, whose mouth was already crammed full of dough balls, looked a bit shifty.

Mom picked up her knitting again and said, "Well, I think you should go upstairs and get changed. You'll catch a cold in that damp sweatshirt."

"Now, now, dear!" Dad said, eager as ever to help. "I almost forgot. There's no need to worry! I've got just the thing!" He rummaged around in the white plastic carrier bag he had brought home that morning and pulled out a small, brightly colored packet. "Here you are, Billy," he said, ripping it open and shaking out its contents. "Our company's brand-new T-shirt. You'll be the first to try it on!" He waved it about with a flourish.

"What do you think? Good, huh?"

Bill stared at the T-shirt in shock. "But, Dad, it's bright pink!" he protested in disgust.

"And it's covered in swirly green writing!" added Stacey, pointing to the words "Finn's Fine Fish Foods" daubed across its back.

"And why does it have a picture of a killer whale saying, 'Moo!' on the front?" I asked.

Dad looked at me with pity and chuckled to himself.

"'Moo?' No, no, Ned. It says 'Boo!' The killer whale is saying 'Boo!' It's a joke." He tapped his finger on the side of his nose. "It's what we in the trade call a *marketing ploy*. It's there to catch the attention of the public!" Looking a bit sheepish, he coughed and said, "You see, with all the excitement, I haven't had time to tell you, but we've won the contract at the zoo to feed their new killer whale—you know, the one they rescued from that Hollywood film set recently? Well, it arrives next week—along with their new Marine Life Manager—and I thought it would be a good idea to advertize that fact. After all, what's good enough for a magnificent beast like a killer whale is good enough for any old fishbowl."

Dad was on a roll. He leaned forward, ready to share his enthusiasm. "No one should waste an opportunity for a bit of promotion. So I thought it would be great if you kids could go to the aquarium and hand out these T-shirts with some free samples of my fish food. Look," he said, picking up the T-shirt, "the zoo's given the old aquarium a state-of-the-art makeover—you can see it on the back of the T-sh . . ."

His voice trailed off as he studied the shirt more closely. Then he shouted, "That Geoff! I'll murder him! No wonder these were so cheap! All that crazy man can think about are his cows! Look at that mistake!" He stabbed his finger at the word "Moo" on the T-shirt he was holding. "He's printed the wrong word! I'm going to kill him!"

"Oh, Dan," Mom wailed, her needles clacking together at double speed. "Tell me you didn't use Geoff to print your T-shirts?"

Dad nodded, dumbly.

Geoff—or Goofy Geoff, as he is known locally—is Dad's best friend and the worst printer in town. He can't spell, he can hardly see, and he's obsessed with cows in the same way that Dad is with fish. He sneaks pictures of them on to everything he prints. The whole town is littered with signs and billboards decorated for no good reason with pictures of Holstein cows and Jersey calves. Only Dad would have hired someone like Geoff to print a T-shirt. But then, Dad *is* a fashion zero. He hasn't got a clue when it comes to clothes. He's the only man I know who thinks "smart casual" means wearing a salmon tie with a polo shirt.

"Well, I'm sorry, Dad, but there's no way I'll be seen in one of those!" sneered Stacey, flipping her hair.

"No, no, of course not," said Mom reassuringly,

starting on another ball of wool. Goodness knows who she was making this sweater for, but I figured it would be on their back by dinnertime. "I'm sure we can do something to sort this all out. We'll just ask Geoff to print some more. We might even be able to change their color a bit." She looked at Dad. "I know pink is really eye-catching, but it doesn't really go with Stacey's red hair, does it?"

Stacey ground her teeth. "*Auburn*, not red," she muttered, tossing her carrot-red mane everywhere.

Mom ignored her and turned back to Dad. "Now, tell me, Dan. How many T-shirts did you say you had printed?"

Dad looked in the air and then down at his toes. "Twenty," he said casually. "Yup, twenty would be about right."

"Well, then," said Mom, smiling, "there's nothing to worry about, is there? We'll just get another twenty printed."

"No," said Dad, pushing his toe into the kitchen rug and refusing to meet Mom's eye. "I don't think you understand. I meant twenty—er, *thousand*. I've got twenty thousand T-shirts printed with the word 'Moo!' sitting in the garage. Do you think I might have over-ordered?"

Chapter 8
JOE
THE
BULLY

The rest of the week passed in a haze. Only Bill seemed happy. In fact, he seemed remarkably cheerful. He kept disappearing for hours on end and coming back with a big grin on his face, smelling faintly of rotten fish. I was very suspicious. Try as I might, I could not figure out what he was up to or where he went. He'd vanish into thin air. No one else noticed. But then, we were all pretty busy trying to work out what to do with the truckload of misprinted T-shirts that Dad had stashed in the garage.

Mom and Dad couldn't bear the thought of

upsetting Geoff by asking him to print the T-shirts a second time, especially when Dad told Mom that Geoff had done them so cheaply as a favor. He had printed them as part of a special T-shirt deal he was doing for the annual Cattlebury Cattle Show. What made it even worse was that he simply couldn't see what was wrong with them. In fact, Geoff was convinced that everyone at the cattle show or the zoo would buy one.

We tried to persuade Mom and Dad to burn them, or at least take them to the dump, but Mom wouldn't hear of it. There were too many of them and, anyway, she hates to waste anything. Her view was that if Dad was in a mess, it was up to us to help him sort it out. She wouldn't hear any arguments. We were to go to the zoo that weekend and:

1. Try to get rid of (sorry, "hand out") as many of Dad's crummy T-shirts and bags of Fish Chips as we could.

And (much worse):

2. I had to watch Bill.

I mean honestly, why me? Why not Stacey? But there was nothing I could do. Bill smiled his most angelic smile and promised to be good. He said he couldn't wait to go to the zoo and that he was really looking forward to seeing the new aquarium. He even insisted on packing the backpack for Mom. Looking back, I should  have realized that he was up to something. By the time I did, it was way, way too late.

Saturday morning turned out to be every bit as bad as we feared.

Dad made us get up really early so we wouldn't miss a single customer at the zoo. We didn't mind very much. The earlier we got there, the sooner we could get away. But we hadn't considered Dad.

Although he was too shy (or embarrassed) to go out and sell the T-shirts himself, he couldn't help interfering. He kept spying on us from behind bushes and whispering instructions. If anyone looked vaguely interested, he would hiss loudly at us and wave his arms around like a madman. But as soon as anyone read the slogan on the T-shirts, they'd laugh and walk away. No one was even remotely interested in taking a sample of the fish food.

In the end, even Dad gave up. Sighing deeply, he left for home. He looked so dejected and miserable that it was difficult not to feel sorry for him. We decided to stick around and hope that things improved. Otherwise, what was Dad going to do with all his worthless T-shirts?

We were just trying to figure out a solution to the problem, when something happened that turned a bad situation even worse. Joe Blagg, the school bully, arrived.

My heart sank. Joe is the kind of boy who's nobody's friend and everyone's enemy. He's a greedy, lazy delinquent with sharp, beady eyes that peek out from behind a thick mop of unwashed hair. Even the teachers are frightened of him because his mother has a habit of hitting them with her handbag if they 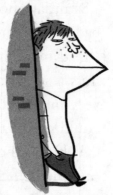 ever dare to complain about his behavior. I had spent all year avoiding Joe's attention, mainly by keeping out of his way. But as soon as I saw the glint in his eye that morning, I knew my time was up.

"Well, well, well," he drawled thickly through a mouthful of food. He sauntered up to us. "If it isn't the three thick Finns." He laughed at his joke. "Let's see, what does your T-shirt say?" He leaned forward and stared at my chest. "Oh, yes, I see: 'Moo!' Ha! Ha! That's got to be a misprint. But then you've probably been to Goofy Geoff the printer. It's all your kind can afford! *Moo!* Well, Red," he sneered, turning to Stacey and smirking, "I suppose it's better to turn into a cow than a carrot top—but you can tell your dad from me that I think his T-shirts are a load of old bull!"

He stopped short and suddenly had an idea. You could tell when Joe Blagg had an idea because it lit up his face, like a single lightbulb in a blackened room.

"A load of old bull—I made a joke! Moo—cow—bull! Geddit?!" He collapsed in a fit of laughter.

I gritted my teeth and struggled not to speak. In the end, it was Bill who cracked first. Dad might be eccentric, but no one criticizes him in front of us and gets away with it. Unable to restrain himself, Bill ran forward and tried to kick Joe in the shins. I joined him from behind. Stacey, angry at being called "Red" and "Carrot Top" when everyone knows she is, in reality, a blonde, yelled encouragement. Joe dodged us and then, sticking two fat fingers in his mouth, gave a piercing whistle. Instantly, as though out of thin air, his two henchmen, Thrasher and Crasher, appeared. We were in big trouble. Between them, those three had the strength of a hammerhead shark. We ducked and ran.

Joe, Thrasher, and Crasher lumbered after us all over the zoo: up by the chimpanzees, down by the giraffes, and along past the snake house. Finally, we ended up at the aquarium. There was simply nowhere else to go—and no way out except the way we had come. The aquarium itself was a large, round, steep-sided tank surrounded by a semicircle of concrete steps and uncomfortable plastic seats. There was a battered shovel and a pile of stones to one side of the pool where someone was obviously trying to create a new water feature. On the other, there was a large truck with a huge container on the back.

Panting and out of breath, we crouched behind the aquarium seats and waited for Joe and his cohorts to come around the corner. But they never arrived. When it was clear that they'd given up the chase—presumably distracted by the hot dog stand next to the penguin tank—I sat up and tried to work out what to do. I was pretty sure that Joe, Thrasher, and Crasher would wait for us at the exit to the zoo. Our best chance was to sit it out in the aquarium and hope that, in time, the bullies would give up and go home. Even Bill, who can't stand having to wait for anything, thought it was the best plan.

Half an hour passed.

Then another.

Bill began to run out of patience. "I'm hungry," he complained. "Very, *very* hungry."

In an effort to distract him, I pointed out a badly printed sign nearby. It said:

COMING SOON!
KYLIE THE KILLER WHALE
SHE IS 32 FEET LONG, HAS 48 TEETH, AND WEIGHS 9 TONS

In the bottom left-hand corner, you could just see a tiny picture of an Aberdeen Angus bull wearing a red ribbon. I sighed. Goofy Geoff had been at it again.

Stacey was unimpressed.

"*Kylie*," she cried in disgust. "*Kylie!* What kind of name is that for a killer whale?"

Bill nodded. "I agree," he said, peering into the empty water. "Kylie will be bored and hungry—just like me." He turned around and looked at me with a set of beseeching eyes, like a puppy that hadn't been fed for a week. "N-e-e-e-e-e-d f-o-o-o-o-d," he whined. "Are you sure you don't have any food left? I'm starving."

I groaned. Since we had arrived at the zoo, Bill had demolished two bags of chips, a chocolate bar, and some moldy toffees that had been stuck to the inside of my pocket. Anything he hadn't eaten had been devoured by my sister, Miss Chocoholic herself. I searched around in the backpack to check if there was anything I'd missed.

"Nope! Sorry! You're out of luck," I said. "All I've got left are Dad's bags of fish food."

Bill didn't mind. He wasn't picky. Before I had time to think, Bill seized his chance, grabbing a couple of bags and ripping them open.

"You can't eat that stuff!" I protested. "You don't know what's in it."

"Too late," mumbled Bill, his eyes shining above

his bulging cheeks.

I stared at him, unable to believe how stupid he was being. But before I could come up with a suitably crushing comment, I was distracted by a noise from behind. A tall woman was wobbling her way up the slope on a pair of impossibly high-heeled shoes, accompanied by several officials. She was carrying a megaphone and was obviously not in a good mood. I was just trying to figure out what was going on, when Bill touched me on the arm.

"Uh-oh, Ned," he said, "I think I feel a little fishy."

"What do you mean?" I asked him. But before Bill could answer, there was a sudden flash, bang, and whizz, and somehow, in some way, my six-year-old brother dove into the aquarium. Bill had disappeared and there, in the water, was a grubby gray cod with an unmistakable grin on its face and a single golden curl coming out of the top of its head.

Chapter 9
BILL IN TROUBLE!

I couldn't believe what had just happened.

One moment, my brother was standing next to me, whining about being hungry. The next, there was a cod swimming happily around in the tank and grinning just like Bill—and looking *remarkably* like the one that had jumped out of our fishpond and slapped me in the face. Stacey and I rushed to the side of the pool and peered in, our mouths open in shock.

"Look at me!" cried the bizarre-looking cod (apparently fish that were once boys can talk). "Aren't I great?" He did a backflip. If ever a cod could look smug, this one did.

Great? I simply couldn't believe my eyes. "Bill!

What's happened to you?" I shouted. "What on earth have you done?"

"He's turned into a f-iiii-sh!" cried Stacey, and then she burst into tears. "Do something!" she ordered me. "Change him back!"

I rolled my eyes. I don't mean to be unhelpful or anything, but changing a younger brother back from being a cod into a boy is not part of my day-to-day routine. What exactly did she expect me to do?

Bill, of course, didn't seem the least bit concerned. "Oh, don't worry! Watch this," he called out cheerfully, doing a double somersault out of the water. "This is fantastic. You have to come in, Stacey, the water's great! All you need to do is shovel a couple of handfuls of Dad's fish food into your mouth!"

Stacey cheered up immediately. "Okay," she said, "I will. How many bags do you think I'll need?" And she ran back to rummage through the backpack.

I acted fast. "Look," I snapped, grabbing it from her. "There is NO way I'm going to allow you to become a fish, too. One cod in the family is quite enough, thank you."

"It's not fair," Stacey wailed, as usual. "Why do you and Bill always have more fun than I do?"

"Fun?" I cried in disbelief. This wasn't fun; this was classic Bill—Trouble with a capital T. "This is a disaster! How on earth are we going to explain this to Mom? I can just see us going home and saying, 'Mom, you know how you asked us to take Bill to the zoo and make sure he didn't get into any trouble? Well, we had a great time, except that Bill accidentally turned into a fish—we left him swimming around in a large tank that is about to become a home for a not-so-friendly killer whale.'"

I stared at Bill in horror. What would happen if we couldn't change him back? Or if Joe and his buddies came around the corner and found out what was going on? I tried to keep calm. At the very least, I had to get Bill out of the tank. I just needed to work out how.

My first instinct was to ask for help. The seats around the aquarium were beginning to fill up— but how could I explain what had happened? Everyone would think we were insane! No, I had to face the facts. Bill was in trouble—and it was up to me to sort it out.

Looking around, I saw a bucket at the bottom of the steps. "Okay, Bill," I said, trying to sound reassuring. "Leave it to me! I'll get you out of there just as soon as I can! Whatever you do, keep calm!"

"Take your time, bro!" said Bill, concentrating more on his triple somersault than on what I was saying.

I picked up the bucket and, ignoring my fear of water, tried to reach over the side of the pool to dangle it into the tank. But I wasn't quite tall enough to reach over. And Stacey wasn't either.

"Stacey!" I yelled, thinking fast. "Take this bucket and guard it with your life. I'm going to find a ladder. Now, whatever you do, *don't leave Bill alone.*"

Stacey, who had stopped crying, clutched the bucket and tried to look brave. And then, just when I thought things couldn't get any worse, they did. There was a loud crackling noise overhead and the sound system buzzed into action.

"Ahem! Ladies and gentlemen," boomed a loud, high-pitched female voice, "we here at the zoo are proud to present for the very first time and two days earlier than advertised—all the way from Hollywood, California—the arrival of that terrifying and death-defying monster—Kylie the killer whale!"

And with those words, the underwater gates of the aquarium slid open and thirty-two feet of black-and-white killer whale entered the tank.

Chapter 10
RESCUE!

Let's recap:

1. Bill, my brother, has turned into a cod and is swimming around in a large aquarium.
2. He has just been joined there by Kylie, a very dangerous killer whale. Kylie looks hungry. My brother is the only food available.
3. The sole way I can save Billy-the-fish is to turn him back into Billy-the-boy. Unfortunately, I don't have a clue how to do this.

4. Conclusion: Kylie is going to think Bill is her fish food and I am going to . . .

PPPPPAAAAAAAAANNNNNNIIIIIC!!!

"Quick, pass me the bucket!" I yelled at Stacey. Grabbing her shoulders with both hands, I hauled myself up onto her back and leaned over the rail. By standing on Stacey's shoulders, I could just get the bucket into the water. Stacey, protesting loudly, staggered around trying to balance my weight.

"Stop squishing my head!" she moaned. But I didn't care. Our brother could be a pain in the neck, but I didn't want him to end up as Kylie's dinner.

"Keep swimming!" I yelled at Bill.

"I am!" he shouted back. And he was. In fact, I have never seen a fish swim so fast. He was diving, pirouetting, jumping, and flipping. But it was no good. Kylie, who obviously relished the game, had noticed him and was closing in fast. I could sense it would not be long before Bill ran out of energy.

"Try and distract her," I shouted, as I failed once again to catch Bill in the bucket when he shot past.

"How?" my brother asked breathlessly as he

narrowly dodged one of Kylie's fins.

"I don't know," I snapped back, irritated. "Tell her some jokes, ask her about herself. If you can look like a fish, maybe you can speak like a fish, too!" The gathering crowd was having a ball. They thought we were the first act and were beginning to clap and cheer.

There was another crackling noise from above. Again, the bossy lady's voice began to address the crowd that was now rushing to take their seats.

"Welcome, welcome, everyone—boys and girls, moms and dads," she said. There was a pause and then the sound of a fingernail tapping the microphone. "Come on now, hurry up," she continued, a little annoyed. "There's room for everyone. Well, there would be, if you were slim and beautiful like me—but then," there was a sigh, "I suppose it would be impossible to be so perfect . . . I have just been to HOLLYWOOD, you know, to collect this stinking—I mean, uh, this *beautiful* killer whale . . . " She coughed and regained her composure, continuing in honeyed tones. "So, *please* take your time—take all the time you need to get to your seats—BUT JUST DON'T TAKE ALL DAY!" she snapped.

There was another pause as the speaker struggled to control her temper again.

"Now, today is the big day—AND NO, IT'S *NOT* MY FAULT THAT IT'S EARLY— HONESTLY, TRYING TO GET ANYTHING DONE ON A TIMETABLE IN THIS CRAZY COUNTRY IS IMPOSS—" She broke off as her voice became increasingly shrill.

"Of course, I mean that due to unforeseen circumstances, we are *thrilled* to announce, two days earlier than we thought possible, the arrival of Kylie, the killer whale, our great star of the Hollywood screen—BUT NOT AS BIG A STAR

AS ME, DONNA MEZZWEME, THE MAGNIFICENT MANAGER, THE ZEALOUS ZOOKEEPER, THE . . . THE . . . THE ACNE OF AQUARIUMS!"

There was a puzzled silence and a reluctant ripple of applause. Stacey and I weren't the only ones around that aquarium staring at each other in amazement. Was she really comparing herself to a face full of zits? But before we could say anything, the loudspeaker system burst once more into life.

"Goodness me!" said the voice excitedly. "Kylie seems very lively. Would you look at that whale GO? You'd think, after a transatlantic flight, she'd be a little jet-lagged, like me . . . "

There followed a hastily smothered yawn and an awkward cough. It was then that Donna Mezzweme noticed us, still desperately trying to catch Bill in the bucket.

"What are those children doing down there!" she snapped. "I don't believe it! Are they trying to play with our killer whale?"

There was a gasp of disapproval from the crowd as everyone in the audience turned to look at Stacey and me.

Then the voice barked out, all friendliness

vanished: "Attendants! Attendants, GRAB THOSE KIDS! Get them out of there!"

The crowd turned against us and leaned forward, pointing their fingers and craning their necks to see what would happen next. Somehow, I didn't think now was the right time to explain that we weren't *playing* with Kylie—we were in a Finn-to-fin struggle for Bill's life. And it wasn't clear which Finn would win. Bill was jumping here, there, and everywhere. I was sloshing around with a bucket, and Stacey was staggering up and down the edge of the pool trying to hold me upright. Suddenly, some of the spectators realized what was going on.

They started to cheer and stand up to get a better look. The buzz of interest grew louder. But Stacey ·

and I were only interested in getting Bill into our grimy bucket. We only had seconds left to save our brother from the jaws of death. As the attendants arrived, I saw Kylie's great tooth-filled jaw rise up from the water, ready for the kill. With one last effort, Bill dashed toward us and leaped in a great arc into the air. The crowd gasped. Everyone, including the attendants, held their breath. There was an enormous splash, and Bill landed safely in our pail. A huge cheer went up. We had done it! Bill was safe! Shaking with fright, Stacey and I collapsed on the ground in a heap, clutching the bucket between us.

"Don't worry," panted Billy-the-fish from the bucket. "Kylie's not angry, she's just laughing. I took your advice and told her a joke."

I stared down at him blankly.

"I asked her what you would get if you crossed a duck-billed platypus with a *plonker* like my sister." He waited for us to answer and when we didn't, he continued, "A duck-billed plonker-puss, of course!"

Bill, still in the bucket, roared with laughter.

Sometimes, I really think I could *kill* my brother.

Chapter 11 FAME

You might think things would have improved at that point, but after we had rescued Bill, they became even more difficult.

Bill, thankfully, had somehow remained in the bucket of water. Stacey, who had landed in a heap underneath me, was rolling around on the ground with my foot in her face (a mistake, I swear). The crowd was clapping and cheering.

None of this impressed Donna Mezzweme. She came tottering toward us on her high-heeled shoes. Her dyed yellow hair was piled up on her head in a bun that wobbled as she walked. She was wearing the largest pair of dark sunglasses I had ever seen, even though it was an overcast day. Her face was purple with anger.

"What on earth do you think you're doing?" she snapped, eyeing us suspiciously.

I sighed. It was not going to be easy to explain our way out of this mess.

"Sorry," I muttered. "We were just saving this, um, cod."

"Saving a cod?" she repeated in disbelief. She peered into the bucket, unable to lean down very far because her skirt was so tight. Bill smirked and did his best to look appealing. Donna Mezzweme was not impressed. "Yuuuck," she sniffed, stepping backward in disgust. "I've never seen such an ugly fish." She paused and jabbed a perfectly painted red talon at Bill. "Is that *hair* sticking out of its head?"

Bill stuck his tongue out at her and, as she jumped back in alarm, she was distracted by a shout from the crowd.

"That boy's a hero!" someone cried. "He saved that tiny fish from the killer whale. Let's give him a round of applause." Everyone started to clap. And the next thing I knew, a reporter from the local newspaper had rushed up to take a picture of us.

"Well, well," tittered Donna insincerely, "I suppose everything has turned out for the best." Pushing her sunglasses to the top of her head, she patted her hair into place, tugged at her skirt, and reapplied a thick layer of lipstick. Striking a pose, she pouted and smiled smugly at the camera. Then she hissed under her breath, "Now, look, my name is Donna Mezzweme. I am the new marine life manager. And *you* ..." she sneered as she read our T-shirts, "*you* must be Dan Finn's children. Well, I don't care how good his Fish Chips are, you can tell your dad from me that HE'S LOST HIS CONTRACT and that I *never* want to see you or your cod near Kylie again."

She didn't have to worry. Stacey, Bill, and I had had enough whales to last three lifetimes. It had been a tiring day. Nodding goodbye to the reporter, and with the cheers from the crowd ringing in my ears, I picked up my brother in the bucket and quietly trudged home with Stacey. My head was buzzing with worries:

1. What was Dad going to say when he discovered he'd lost his contract to feed the killer whale?
2. How would Mom react when she read all about this in the local paper?

And above all:

3. **What were we going to do with Bill?**
4. How long could we hide him in a bucket?
5. And how on earth were we going to turn him from a fish back into a boy?

HIDDEN DEPTHS

When we reached home, we had our first piece of luck in a week. The house was empty. Mom, thinking Dad was with us at the zoo, had gone out.

> *Gone to get my hair cut*
> *Back at one*
> *Love, Mom*
> *xxx*

"Quick!" I shouted to Stacey. "Go and fill the bath!" Stacey, for once, didn't argue. She charged up the stairs and turned on the cold water full blast.

"Ouch!" went Bill, as we turned the bucket

upside down and dumped him into the water. "Watch out for my nose!" He swam without enthusiasm up and down the bath a few times. "It's not nearly as much fun as the aquarium," he said, sulking. "The water's too cold, and it's too shallow to dive—"

"Well, at least you're not sharing your bath with a killer whale," I snapped back, exasperated.

"That's true," replied Bill. "Although I have to say we got along pretty well, considering." He paused and then said, "I know. If I can't dive, I'll try something else." And  before I knew what was happening, he had flipped up onto his tail and was ricocheting from one side of the bath to the other, stirring up water. "Hey, wheelies!" he cried happily.

"Oh, Bill, you are so clever!" cried Stacey, clapping her hands. "You've turned the bath into a jacuzzi!"

"A ja-cod-zi is more like it!" laughed Bill. "This is great!"

I groaned. Things were bad enough without Bill

making terrible fish jokes. He was beginning to sound just like Dad. And as for the bathroom, there was water everywhere. I bent down onto the floor and tried to mop it up with one of Mom's pink fluffy towels.

"Now look, Your Almighty Codliness," I said, deciding that two can play Fish Puns, "I'll put you back in that bucket if you don't stop messing around." I wrung the towel out over the bath and eyed him suspiciously. "Are you *really* sure this is the first time you've ever turned into a fish?"

Bill ignored my question. "Hey! This is the most fun I've had in ages. And don't worry, I'm sure I'll turn back into a boy at some point. I just need to wait for the effect of the food to wear off, don't I? To tell you the truth, I think I can sort of feel it happening now."

Stacey and I peered at Bill closely. He definitely seemed to be getting hairier, and some of his scales were coming off in the bath. He also appeared to be growing.

Stacey laughed and started to splash Bill. But I felt more than a bit annoyed. It didn't seem right that Bill was taking the situation so lightly. How was he so sure that he wasn't going to remain a cod-ugly fish for the rest of his life? As usual, it was up to me to sort out this mess. I sat down on the bathroom stool and started to rifle through the fish food samples in my backpack.

"These look the same as the stuff Dad normally sells," I muttered, "only the wrappers are a different color. They're not very clearly labeled." I tore open a packet and squinted at its contents suspiciously. "Nothing strange there," I said, shaking it. I sniffed it cautiously. It seemed to smell okay. I opened another bag. It was exactly the same. I laid both bags on the side of the bath while I rummaged around some more.

"Well, Bill, it looks like you're right. There's nothing to do but see what happens. We'll simply have to wait for you to turn back into a boy. I just hope it doesn't take too long. That bathroom lock still hasn't been fixed—anyone could walk in. All I can say is, thank goodness Mom's out. How long do you think it will be before she gets back?"

"Not long enough," Stacey said in a hollow voice, looking through the bathroom window. "Guess who's walking up the driveway?"

"Quick!" I yelled to Stacey. *"Lock the door!"*

Stacey tried, but it was no good. The lock was

completely busted, and however much she tried to force it, it would not jam shut. Bill started to panic.

"NED! Ned! Help me!" he begged, dashing up and down the bath. "Hide me! Put me somewhere! Mom will go crazy if she sees me like this!"

"But where?" I cried, trying hard to keep calm. Bill had grown even bigger. "I can't put you in the bucket, and you're too big to fit down the toilet!"

"But she'll *kill* me if she catches me like this!"

"Well—maybe you should have thought about that before you started fooling around with Dad's fish food," I snarled.

But Bill was right. Mom was going to explode. And not just with Bill. When she discovered that her youngest son had turned into a fish and played hide-and-seek with a killer whale in public, I figured I would be next in front of the firing squad. She always seemed to think that it was my job to look after Bill. We were both seriously fileted.

"Hello-oo!" trilled Mom from downstairs. "I'm back! Is anyone at home?"

"Ssh!" I whispered. "Don't say anything!"

We held our breath, but we hadn't thought of Mom's supersonic hearing.

"Oh, you're upstairs, are you?" she said. "Well, just

hang on while I bring the groceries in and then I'll come up and see you. I'm dying to show you my new hairdo!" We heard her put down her bags and go back outside to the car.

We were in a fine kettle of fish. I shut my eyes and thought fast.

"Okay," I hissed, dragging up the stool. "Stacey, you sit on this and lean against the door. Wedge your feet against the bathtub, and whatever you do, don't let Mom in!" Before I could say anything else, I heard Mom starting to climb the stairs.

"Billy, Stacey, Neddy!" she called. "Where's Dad? What are you all doing in the bathroom? Are you okay? Did you have fun at the zoo? Did you manage to get rid of any T-shirts?"

No one said a word.

Mom instantly went on red alert. Her voice became much sharper. "Ned, Stacey, Billy? What's going on?" She rapped on the door. "Look," she said, "I know you're in there, so you might as well own up. What are you doing?"

"Um, nothing," I said shakily. "Bill's just taking a bath . . . "

"Taking a bath? Billy? At this time of day?" squawked Mom. "He must be crazy. I can barely get

90

him to take one before bed. Are you sure he's okay?" She rattled the door. Stacey's face was going bright pink with the effort of pushing against it. "And what's wrong with the door? Why can't I get in?"

"Um, don't worry, Mom," I said desperately, "I think the handle's just stiff. And Bill's fine." I laughed. "He just got a little bit wet and . . . um . . . " I fished around for some inspiration and saw Stacey's luminous T-shirt, " . . . some of the dye came off his shirt, so we're giving him a bath . . . "

I wiped my forehead. Sweat was dripping off of me. I wasn't used to lying.

Mom was just about to answer when Dad came home.

"Dan! Dan!" hollered Mom from the other side of the bathroom door. "Billy's taking a bath and the kids are telling me some story about the dye coming off of Geoff's goofy T-shirts! What on earth's been going on? And the bathroom door's jammed. I've told you time and time again about that door!"

Dad mumbled something and came upstairs.

He coughed loudly and said importantly, "Okay, children, stand back! I'm going to push the door hard a couple of times with my shoulder. If it still doesn't budge, I'll run at it from the end of the hallway. Don't panic, now. You'll be out any minute now!"

Don't panic! *Don't panic!* Dad is over six feet tall. There was no way we could hold the door against him. I turned around to Bill.

"Dive!" I cried, pushing him under the water. But he had grown even bigger. The gray bulk of his codlike form was clearly visible under the water. Desperate times call for desperate measures. I grabbed a jar of Mom's favorite pink bubble bath and poured it under the running water.

Stacey gasped. "Oh, no! Not that one, Ned! It's Mom's favorite. It's called Pink Passion. It costs a fortune!"

"Well, if it hides Bill, then it will be worth its weight in gold!" I replied. I swirled the water around. Pink bubbles danced everywhere and clouds of perfume filled the room.

Mom instantly smelled a rat—or should I say fish. She knocked hard on the door. She was no longer sympathetic; she was suspicious.

"Children! Children! What are you doing with my best bath oil? I can smell it from here—do you know how much it costs?"

We all ignored her. So did Dad.

"Stand clear!" he cried from outside, rolling up his sleeves and preparing for his first strike. "I'm coming in!"

THUMP! went the door. Mom yelped. Bill ducked below the water and then bobbed back up almost instantly.

"Yuck!" spluttered Bill, spitting pink bubbles everywhere. "This stuff stinks! You can't possibly think I'm going to hide under this junk."

"Yes, I do!" I hissed, shoving him back down under the water. "This is the only chance we have of saving you from being fried alive by Mom and Dad!"

THUMP! Dad hit the door a second time.

"Ouch!" Stacey said, but she held firm.

I yanked the shower curtain around the bath and accidentally knocked the two open bags of fish food I'd balanced on the side of the bath. They shot up into the air, scattering their contents everywhere. Instantly, Bill—a sucker for free food even in a crisis—jumped out of the water and gobbled it all up.

I stared at him, aghast. "Bill, what have you done now?" I wailed. Surely, not even my crustacean of a brother could have been so stupid as to eat a double dose of Dad's demented fish food? What was he going to turn into this time? An octopus?

Even Bill realized he'd been silly. "Ned," he said in a faint voice. "I don't feel very well. I've got a tummy ache. In fact, I think . . . " His voice trailed off. There was a flash! A bang! And a whizz! And somehow, some way, Billy-the-cod changed back into a boy. Where one moment there had been a large and ugly gray fish with a shock of yellow curly hair, there was now my brother, sitting up to his chin in pink bubbles, butt-naked and covered in gloopy gray slime!

"Bill! B-iii-ll's back!" sobbed Stacey with relief.

I nodded in silence. I was too stunned to speak. How had Bill done it? How had he managed to turn himself back into a boy just like that? I fished out one of the empty chip bags from the water and stared at it blankly. But before I could do any more, Dad rapped on the door.

"Now, children," he said gravely, "watch out! I'm going to run at the door from the end of the hallway! I don't want to hurt you, so stand clear!"

I shot another look at Bill. His hair was covered in greasy gray scales. Thinking quickly, I grabbed Mom's bright pink shower cap and rammed it over his head, just as Dad charged at the door. Caught off guard, Stacey toppled forward off the stool, and Dad and Mom fell into the room.

"Ah, I knew that would do the trick!" said Dad, trying hard not to rub his shoulder. "Just as I thought, the door was jammed . . . " His voice trailed off as he saw Bill. He was sitting bolt upright in a sea of pink bubbles, wearing Mom's fluffy pink shower cap, and covered in what looked like ghoulish-gray face paint.

"What on earth . . . ?" he sputtered, looking at his youngest son. There was silence. Then Mom spoke. "Billy, darling, what have they done to you?"

"US?" Stacey squealed, unable to stand the injustice of it all. "What have WE done to HIM?"

"Don't worry, Mom," I hastily interrupted. "That gray stuff's just one of Stacey's face masks. Bill was experimenting." I lowered my voice. "He thinks he's got pimples—and another lice infestation," I whispered.

Mom closed her eyes in horror.

"Pimples!" cried Dad, whose eyes were bugging.

"And lice? But he's up to his neck in PINK BUBBLES!"

"It's the smell—and the color," I said desperately. "As of today, he really, *really* likes the color pink."

"Yeah, and the school nurse says that lice are particularly allergic to anything pink," Stacey said convincingly. She was enjoying this. "And Bill, um, wants to get in touch with . . . with . . . his feminine side. I think he was inspired," she said, warming to the theme, "by your T-shirts, Dad."

It was all too much for Dad. He gulped and sat down on the side of the bathtub. "My T-shirts?" he whispered faintly. "His feminine side? But he's only six . . ."

"Oh well," said Mom, regaining her powers of speech and trying to put a positive spin on matters, "there's nothing wrong with pink, is there? After all, it's my favorite color! Though next time, Billy, I think you should ask me before you use *all* my best bubble bath!"

Dad pulled himself together. "Yes, yes, your mom's quite right, as always," he said. "Everything in moderation, that's what I say. Things have been really out of hand this past week. Why don't we all take a break? What do you say to all of us spending time together this weekend? We could go to the racetrack? Or do some kickboxing or perhaps go to a soccer match?"

"Wicked!" cried Bill.

Stacey curled her lip in disgust—it's her automatic reaction to any suggestion that doesn't involve her friends, a makeup-buying trip, or a new magazine. I could only nod. I was too shattered to speak. All I knew was that there was no way I was going to tell Mom and Dad what had happened. Instead, I was just going to make sure it never happened again.

Which goes to show you that even good plans can fail.

Chapter 13

FROM BAD TO WORSE

The rest of the weekend was almost normal.

After we had cleaned up Bill and dried out the bathroom, Mom and Dad insisted on us all doing things as a family. Stacey, who's read magazine articles about this sort of thing, told us this was called "bonding" and refused to get excited. But Bill and I had a great time. First we went bowling, then we watched a football game on TV, and on Sunday we played catch at the local park all afternoon. Mom didn't complain once about our muddy shoes, and even Stacey eventually said she enjoyed it (but only after Dad bought her a year's supply of Goopy Gloop Hair Spray and matching silver nail polish). Nothing was said about the T-shirts, Bill's missing clothes, or his nonexistent pimples (although Mom had a good look at his hair and found that he did indeed have lice). No one even mentioned the word zoo.

But every time I looked at my brother I had a terrible sinking feeling in the pit of my stomach.

I couldn't help wondering what Mom and Dad were going to say when they read all about us in the local newspaper. And what Dad would say if he really had lost his contract.

Bill, of course, was completely relaxed. "It's cool!" he said, as we brushed our teeth on Sunday night. "There's *no Finn* to worry about!"

I nearly choked. Bill was becoming disturbingly like Dad.

Stacey was a bit grumpier about it all. She had always wanted to be a star and was worried that she might miss this splendid opportunity for media exposure. "I bet no one notices us," she complained. "It will be just *typical*! There'll probably be a dumb little paragraph tucked away on the inside back page. No one will notice us, no one!"

That sounded good to me. But unfortunately, both Bill and Stacey were wrong.

We were front page news.

"COD SAVE US ALL!" screamed the headline. There was a huge picture of me standing on Stacey's ear, looking white-faced and exhausted. There was also a close-up of Bill in the bucket. I groaned.

Mom, who was eating breakfast when the local paper arrived, stared at it in disbelief.

"I've never read such a load of old codswallop," she said finally. "I can't believe you did all this for a fish. You hate them. Hang on." She paused. "Where's Billy?" There was silence. I scowled into my bowl of cereal and kicked Bill on the foot to keep him quiet. "Do you know," she said, studying the second picture more closely, "I swear that fish looks familiar . . . "

Dad, of course, was thrilled. "Well done," he said, clapping me on the back. "I'm proud of you. Saving a fish from a killer whale, huh! That's good stuff, especially," he said while rubbing his hands, "since you managed to get a picture of our T-shirts on the front page of the daily newspaper. It's excellent publicity. Particularly now that we've lost the contract to feed Kylie." Dad had been very deflated by that news. Donna had sent him a letter in that morning's mail. Fortunately, she had not mentioned us.

But if home was tricky, school was even worse.

First of all, Dad insisted on walking with me across the playground, right up to the entrance. He clasped a copy of the newspaper to his chest, making sure that the photograph faced outward for everybody to see. He kept referring to it in a cheery, breezy manner.

"Ah, Mr. So-and-so, how are you? I'm just taking my son to school . . . Seen the paper? No? Well, we don't want to brag about it, but my son just happens to be on the front page . . . " By the time I reached my locker, my face was as red as a lobster.

But school assembly was even more embarrassing.

"I see today that we have a hero in our midst," said Mr. Peaseby, our principal. He waved a copy of the paper in the air. "On Saturday morning, young Ned Finn of P.S.6 saved a cod from the jaws of a killer whale." There was a murmur of admiration. I went bright red. Then Mr. Peaseby pointed to me and said, "Now, now, come on, Ned. Don't be shy. Why don't you stand up and tell us all about it?"

I struggled to my feet. Somehow I managed to give an extremely edited version of events. But that wasn't enough for Mr. Peaseby.

"Well done, Ned! Well done!" he exclaimed. "But before you sit down, tell us. Who thought up the design for those pink T-shirts? That lime-green swirly writing is just perfect." He looked hard at

the photograph. I tried to ignore the snickers around me. "You see, I think they're really cool." I blinked. Mr. Peaseby obviously shared Dad's fashion sense. "I mean, look at this joke—'*Moo!*'" He laughed heartily. "It's brilliant! Perfect for Mrs. Peaseby's birthday present. In fact, I'll even get one for myself. Do you think I could buy a couple? How much do they cost?"

My head spun. Could he be *serious?* Could anyone really want to pay good money for Dad's goofy gear?

But before I could answer, Bill—always a number cruncher—piped up. "Ten dollars plus two dollars for postage and packaging, with a discount for orders over five."

"Well, I'll take two," smiled the principal. "Anyone else interested?"

To my amazement, a forest of hands went up. I couldn't believe it. We were in business. We were making money. This was great!

Then one hand went up that I wish had not.

It was Joe Blagg.

"Please, sir, can I ask a question?" he asked thickly, through a mouthful of candy.

"Um, yes, I suppose so, Joe. What is it?" said Mr. Peaseby, nervously running his finger along his collar.

"Well, sir, I was thinking that instead of going through all the trouble to decide who should represent the school at next week's Interschool Quiz Championship, why don't we just ask Ned? Seeing that he's so brave and smart and all that! In fact, I have it on good authority that he's been secretly cramming in his room . . . or should I say, his *study*?"

My jaw dropped. *Stacey!* I thought. *Darn* her and her horrible cell phone. Couldn't we keep secrets in our family anymore? I glared at my sister. She went bright pink and avoided my gaze.

Joe, smiling smugly, continued, "We could invite the local press along, too. It would be great publicity for the school! So it wouldn't even matter if he didn't do that well. Just think of the headlines: 'Cod Hero Is Quiz King!'" He paused to let the force of his words sink in. "In fact, if you want," he continued in a reasonable voice, "I could call my dad on my cell phone and ask him to talk to a few journalists today. He's friends with lots of journalists."

That was true. They were constantly calling him to check on his suspicious car deals.

There was silence. The school tournament! I had completely (well, almost completely) forgotten about it. Winning the entertainment system suddenly didn't seem that important. I hadn't looked at a book for two days, and I couldn't remember a single fact. Surely Mr. Peaseby would tell him it was a terrible idea? I tried to keep calm, but all I could feel was the knocking of my knees and the thumping of my heart.

"Ah, yes, Joe," said Mr. Peaseby, tugging nervously at his bow tie. "But, you know, Ned needs a special subject. And it's hardly fair to land one on him at such short notice." He looked away, glad to be able to dismiss the idea.

But Joe wasn't discouraged that easily. "Surely, sir," he said pleasantly, looking directly at me with evil eyes that showed just how deep his jealousy was, "Ned could simply talk about his family's favorite hobby? Lice, or 'nits,' and nit-picking!"

There was a stunned silence and then everyone in the hall burst out laughing. Even the principal allowed himself a smile. But Stacey and I, sticking together once again through thick and Finn, silently vowed to get even with our enemy, Joe. How *dare* he take shots at our family? Just because Bill's head was lice's equivalent of an airport, that did *not* make me an expert on them! I glared at Joe's smirking face, but before I could do anything, the principal coughed, struggling to make himself heard above the din.

"Ah, yes, Joe," he said, rather pompously, "I see you are talking about our great friend the head louse, lice in plural form—nits, as you call them—or, as we should say in Latin: the *Pediculus humanus capitus.*" He chuckled to himself, pleased that he had been given a chance to show off his knowledge. "As you know, they are extremely common, especially in school children. According to a recent survey, approximately seven percent of a community will have head lice at any one time, with six- to twelve-year-olds being the most common sufferers. For some reason, like threadworms, infestations tend to happen . . . "

And with that he was off, droning on and on

about nits, lice, threadworms, tape worms, warts, verrucas, dandruff . . . Our eyes started to glaze over, and, for all I know, we might still have been sitting there now, listening to the lesser-known facts of ingrown toenails and athlete's foot, had Joe not decided to take matters back into his own hands.

He coughed. "Oh, sorry, sir," he apologized. "Of course, I didn't mean nits—I mean, it wouldn't be *fair* to blame the *whole* school's problems on Ned and his younger brother, Bill . . . " It was now Bill's turn to glower at Joe. "Oh, no, sir! I didn't mean nits, I meant *knitting*. Ned's mom's a pro at making those weird—I mean, wonderful—sweaters and socks. I'm sure he'll be able to tell us all about all her balls of wool!"

There was another burst of laughter, and, once more, everyone started to clap. The principal, surprised by the sudden and unexpected turn of events, smiled and nodded in agreement.

"Well done, Joe," he gushed. "Knitting is an excellent subject!"

And so the assembly ended, and everyone sidled out of the hall. I couldn't wait to get out of there. I was in trouble. What did I know about knitting?

Or what did I care, for that matter? No, I was in deep trouble. There was no casting off for me, that was for sure. I knew only one thing: that if I never hated fish before, I hated them now.

Chapter 14
SOLE BROTHERS

It was my brother who sorted it out. He was the sole of resourcefulness.

"Don't worry," he said confidently. "I can help you."

"You?" I said. "How?"

Bill did a double backflip. We were back in the bathroom. My brother, currently in the shape of a fish, was showing off. Stacey and I were sitting on the edge of the bath, watching his latest performance.

"It's easy," he said. "I have a plan." I stared at my brother uneasily. Somehow, whatever this plan was, I didn't think I was going to enjoy my part in it very much. "You see," Bill continued happily, "I've worked out exactly how to turn from a boy into a fish and back again using Dad's fish food . . . only, it's not my discovery, exactly. I got the idea from one of Stacey's science books over there."

Stacey and I both stared in amazement at a pale blue notebook that was half hidden under her overflowing bag of makeup. It was smudged with glittery pink nail polish and decorated with purple love hearts and hundreds of dramatic signatures saying "Stacey Pitt" and "Stacey Depp." It didn't instantly look like the kind of notebook in which you might uncover an earth-shattering scientific discovery.

Stacey looked skeptical. "Are you sure?"

"Oh, yes. Positive! It's a fascinating book, Stacey. You should read it sometime!" Bill, who I had to remind myself was only six, then started to spout out a whole series of number-crunching formulas.

$$\frac{1}{(-2-h)} - \frac{1}{(2-h)} = \frac{2h}{x-2^2}$$

$$3(4) \times 60'000013$$

$$\frac{1}{2}b < \frac{2}{a}a < 0$$

$$67(a_1-1)$$

$$\frac{2^3 + 10 \times 2}{-1013^{10}2}$$

I still don't have a clue what he was going on about, so I've jotted down a few of them just in case they might make some sense to someone else.

Stacey and I listened to our brother in mounting awe.

"Do you know," Stacey's voice was full of wonder, "Mom and Dad are right. If you spent half a second concentrating in class, you could be running the school by now!"

"Yes, but just imagine how dull life would be! I would never have time to do any of this!" cried Bill, leaping in and out of the water. He caught sight of my blank face and started to swim up and down the bath. "I LOVE being a fish! It's so much fun, and it doesn't hurt a bit! In fact, the only annoying thing is not being sure what will happen to my clothes. Sometimes I change back stark naked! Just imagine if someone was passing by. It could be really embarrassing!" He laughed, but stopped when he saw the blank look on my face.

"Look, Ned," he said patiently, "this fish-changing business is really very simple. If I eat two bags of Dad's Super-Strong Fish Chips, I change into a cod. If I eat another two, I change back. If I hold my breath and count backward for the next five

112

seconds I stay small; if I blow outward, I become huge—well, bigger than I am now. It's easy, really," he added modestly. "If I take a risk and don't eat any extra fish food, then I eventually do turn back into a boy, but it takes longer and longer each time and it does leave me smelling a little bit fishy . . ."

I had noticed he was smellier than usual, come to think of it. I had assumed it was Mom's anti-lice shampoo.

Intrigued, Stacey and I decided to test out Bill's theory. And it turned out that Bill was right. It took exactly two bags. Too little, and he ended up as a fish with yellow hair; too much, and he ended up as a boy with fins. Each time he changed, there was a flash! A  bang! And a whizz! But it never seemed to hurt him, however many times he did it. Thankfully, Dad's other fish food packets—the ones for use in homes and aquariums—had no effect on Bill at all. When he munched those, Bill stayed exactly the same—a somewhat annoying, awkward boy.

I sighed uneasily. "This is all well and good, you know, but it's not going to stop me from making an utter fool of myself in the tournament."

The whole school knew that Joe had bet all his allowance on me to fail. But it wasn't just the money. Joe had been going around bullying everyone to make sure they didn't help me. His impersonation of a human sledgehammer was not a pretty sight.

Bill smiled from the bath. "Don't worry," he said, trying to reassure me. "I've told you—I have a cunning plan."

Just at that moment, the doorbell rang. Bill, swallowing exactly the right quantity of Super-Strong Fish Chips, swiftly turned back into a boy and tidied up the bathroom while Stacey and I ran to the stairs to see who was there. Mom opened the door, and we all got a shock. There, wearing huge sunglasses and hiding behind a large, ragged, and strangely familiar-looking bunch of flowers, teetered Ms. Donna Mezzweme, the marine life manager from the zoo.

"Ah, Mrs. Finn, I presume," she said, thrusting the flowers into Mom's hands. "These are for you."

"Thank you," our mother spluttered. Donna

Mezzweme swept past her into the front hall. She smiled, or at least tried to. Somehow it looked like a rather nasty grimace.

"I wouldn't get too excited by them." Her laugh was chilling. "I found them in your front garden. I always think handpicked flowers are the best, don't you?" Without waiting for Mom to answer, she dramatically swept off her sunglasses and started to tap the toe of one of her high-heeled shoes on the floor.

"Hmm, just as I thought," she said, looking around the room. "Scruffy and unkempt—I mean *fancy* and *well kept*, Mrs. Finn!" she recovered, and went on. "You might, Mrs. Finn, be wondering why I have bothered to visit you in this dump—I mean, in your charming house." She looked around the hall, curling her lip. "Well, I am here to personally congratulate your delightful children on their wonderful act of bravery—and to see their cod! EVERYONE is asking about them. EVERYONE wants to see that fish. So, *where* are the brats—I mean sprats? And, more importantly—" she broke off and thrust her nose straight into Mom's face through the flowers, "WHERE is that *cod*?"

Mom, who had also been trying to get this information out of us, was taken by surprise.

Flustered and struggling hard to be polite, she stammered, "W—well, the children are upstairs, I think . . . but I don't know if their fish is—"

"No matter," cried Donna Mezzweme, heading for the staircase. "If that fish is in the house, I'll sniff it out."

Upstairs, Bill, Stacey, and I gasped. What were we going to do? We didn't have a cod, let alone one we could give to Donna. The only cod we knew had two legs, a head, and no tail and was currently crouched beside me in the shape of my brother, Bill.

It was too late to think of anything, for at that moment, Donna Mezzweme tripped over us and fell flat on the ground. She had put her dark glasses back on and hadn't noticed that we were huddled by the banister.

"What the—?" she spluttered furiously, scrambling up onto her hands and knees.

She glared malevolently. "I should have known it would be your fault," she snarled. "Goodness, how I *hate* children. Now," she said, grabbing me by the ear, "if you know what is good for you, SHOW ME THAT COD!"

"Um, it's in the ornamental pond, in the garden," I blurted out, with what I thought was a stroke of genius.

"Well, take me there at once!" retorted the enraged Donna, letting go of me.

We stood up, but something caught Donna's eye. It was the notice on my old (now Stacey's new) bedroom door. Stacey, stubborn to the last, had defied Mom and refused to take it down. The marine life manager went over and read it closely.

"Hoooow interesting," said Ms. Mezzweme. "Fish farmers, eh? Super-Strong Fish Chips for . . ." she caught her breath, "*Scarce Sea Fish* . . . Then THIS notice must refer to an important new type of fish food—one that Dan—your dad," she smiled at us, "HAS SOMEHOW COMPLETELY FORGOTTEN TO TELL ME ABOUT! Ha! We'll see about that. Now SHOW ME YOUR ROOM!"

We had no choice. Donna flung open the door, strode in, and tripped a second time, straight into a pile of my dirty underwear and unwashed socks.

"Yuck!" she cried, scrambling about. "Help! Get me out of here!"

We couldn't, even if we had wanted to. We were laughing too much. Furious, Donna tried to get back onto her feet. But the heels of her shoes had become trapped in the neck hole of one of my undershirts, and she fell over again as soon as she stepped forward. Angry and humiliated, she started chucking pants, T-shirts, and socks at us. One sock landed on the lampshade, another T-shirt on my bunk bed. By the time she reached my wardrobe she was out of breath and had broken two of her bright red talons. That didn't stop her from trying to pry open the wardrobe door, despite the fact that it was jammed right against the bunk beds, just as Dad had intended. Shaking with rage, she started kicking the wardrobe and thumping the door with her hands. She was making such a terrible noise that Mom came pounding up the stairs.

"And just what," she said, in a voice that could cut ice, "*exactly* do you think you are doing, Ms. Mezzweme? And why do you have a pair of Ned's dirty underpants hanging from your sunglasses?"

Donna was disconcerted. "Oh, um, nothing—I was just looking for the cod!" she stuttered.

"Well, I *don't* think you'll find it in there!" my mother retorted, coming to our rescue. Making an inspired guess, she continued, "I think you'll find it in the garden in the ornamental pond! Stacey, Ned, take Miss Messypants into the garden *at once*—she can leave by the side gate." And with that she nodded curtly to the marine life manager, turned on her heel, and left the room.

There was an awkward silence. Stacey politely beckoned Ms. Mezzweme down the stairs, and we trooped out into the garden in silence. I hung back. My ear was still throbbing from where she had twisted it. Bill had disappeared. I didn't blame him one bit.

The grass around the pond was wet and muddy. Ms. Mezzweme's shoes sank into it, leaving large holes wherever she walked. Soon, her shoes were caked with earth and grass. Ms. Mezzweme was not pleased.

"Ick!" she screeched. "If there's one thing I hate more than children, it's nature! Hasn't anyone in this house heard of decking and concrete?"

We ignored her and reached the pond. I peered down. There, lying next to Goldie-the-goldfish, was Billy-the-cod! Using that brilliant brain of his, Bill had secretly eaten some of Dad's Super-Strong Fish Chips and turned into a cod in order to help us out. I could have hugged him!

I pointed Bill out to Ms. Mezzweme. "Look, there's the cod, just by the lily pad," I said.

Grumbling, Donna Mezzweme bent down carefully. Bill took aim and "Thwack!" he jumped out of the water and hit her straight in the eye. Donna jumped back in alarm, and, as she did so, we all heard the telltale ripping of her particularly tight skirt.

"Owwwwwwwwwwwww! That does it! I've had it!" stormed Donna indignantly. "I only came here to buy your blasted cod. *Some* people," she hissed, "are saying that Kylie's bored, and that I should make her life more *fun!* Of all the ridiculous ideas!" she sniffed. "I mean, let's face it, Kylie's a killer whale, not a cuddly toy! I told them that their precious cod would be eaten in two seconds flat, but no, they tell me that Kylie is different, Kylie is sensitive, Kylie is a Hollywood star and just wants someone to play with . . . "

There was a tense silence as Donna seemed to struggle for words. "I mean, imagine—someone with my international reputation being asked to make sure that great ball of blubber has some fun!" She tossed her hair backward over her shoulder in disgust—her bun had completely fallen apart.

Stacey and I looked at each other, horrified at this monstrous woman, who was obviously interested only in money and fame. Then the blood in our veins froze as she continued, more quietly but with an edge of evil in her voice.

"If you ask me, there was something very fishy about that fish. If you ask me . . . " There was a pause as she eyed us strangely. "And exactly *where* is your brother Bill?" We stared blankly at her, but she knew she was onto something. There was a further pause while Stacey and I swallowed hard, before Donna Mezzweme said, "Hmm. Can't answer, can you? Well, don't worry, *I'll* find out!" Then she turned on her muddy heel, swept out of the side gate, and started her car.

Which was unfortunate, because at that moment, Dad drove, at top speed, into the yard.

Donna, who wasn't concentrating, drove straight into the wall to avoid him. There was a bang, a crash, a thud, and a tinkle as her car fell apart around her. Donna was uninjured, but her car was a complete and utter wreck.

Mom, trying to hide her satisfaction, hurried out to help. "I know just where you can find a replacement! Try Mr. Blagg. He's well-known around here—in fact, he's got quite a reputation."

And that's how Donna Mezzweme came to buy the cheapest and junkiest car she could from the cheapest and junkiest car dealer in town. And while she was there, guess what? She overheard Joe Blagg discussing with his dad his bet that I would lose the Interschool Quiz Championship.

Donna, who had been face down in my dirty underwear, had been walloped by a cod, and had demolished her car in our driveway, was desperate to get us back. As interested as ever in making a quick buck, she eagerly put all her spare cash on me losing the competition.

When I heard this—Joe dropped it casually into the conversation at breaktime one day—I felt sicker than ever. Bill reassured me once again. But I still wasn't convinced by his plan.

"Don't worry," he said. "It will be easy. I'll turn into a fish, then you can take me into the quiz in a fishbowl as your lucky mascot. The girls will all have their Beanie Babies and lucky shells, believe me. I've got a great memory. If you help me learn the facts, I'll be able to whisper the answers to you from the bowl. No one will suspect a thing. Nothing can go wrong."

I had to admit that it was a smart plan. Bill had the best memory of anyone I knew. If he could help me, I had a real chance of winning the tournament. Yes, strictly speaking, we would be cheating, but what choice did we have? At least this way, we would defeat that bully Joe Blagg and get back at Donna Mezzweme. Everyone would be grateful—and no one would ever guess the truth.

Which just goes to show that while I knew very little about fish, I knew even less about humans.

Chapter 15
DOUBLE SPEAK

The day of the Interschool Quiz Championship dawned bright and cheery.

I felt about as cheery as a can of sardines.

My last hope—that Mom and Dad would ban me from being in the tournament when they heard that the first prize was a PlayStation and surround-sound entertainment system—came to nothing. Far from being disapproving, they were thrilled. It was just typical. There I was in urgent need of a bit of harsh, undeserved Victorian discipline (such as being banned from taking part in the competition by rigid, humorless parents who disapproved of any form of fun), when said parents promptly underwent a total attitude bypass. I couldn't believe it! After going on and on about how television and computers were the twin evils of our modern age, here they were promising me their full support and telling me (repeatedly) how great I was to even have had the guts to enter the quiz.

In fact, this is what Dad said:

"If you win I'll surf the Internet for a fishy game and we can have some quality time together."

Mom was even worse!

"Don't worry—I'm really looking forward to watching educational documentaries with you on your surround-sound home cinema."

If you ask me, it was a classic case of PA (Parental Amnesia) or DS (Double Speak)—my term for the chasm between what parents say their offspring are supposed to do and think, and what they actually say, do, and think themselves.

Now, I have done some research among my

friends and apparently PA/DS syndrome affects all parents, but my parents are definitely gold medalists in the sport. In fact, it affects them *so* badly and is *so* irritating that, if you don't mind, I am just going to take time out here to explain why I think it should be banned. *(On the other hand, if you want to skip ahead to the next part of the story and miss out on my rant, just hop to page 129, and I'll see you there!)*

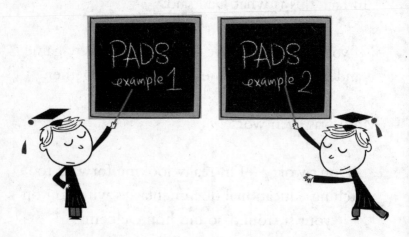

PARENTAL AMNESIA OR DOUBLE SPEAK (PADS)

PADS Classic Example Number One: FOOD

What parents say:

1. Do not snack or eat between meals.
2. Do not taste food while you are cooking.
3. Always eat the food on your plate, including the vegetables.

What parents do:

1. Every time they go into the kitchen, they open the fridge door and (absent-mindedly) cut a chunk of cheese for themselves (Mom), or nibble at a bit of leftover lunch (Dad).
2. When cooking, Mom and Dad always taste the food.
3. On Christmas Day or at Gran's, Dad never eats his brussels sprouts. He feeds them to the dog instead. So does Mom.

ACTUALLY, I MUST ADMIT... I DON'T REALLY LIKE THEM EITHER...

Ring any bells? Well, if not, try my second example, which is even more sinister.

PADS Classic Example Number Two: SUNBATHING

What parents say:
1. Don't go into the sun—or, go only if totally smothered in sunscreen.
2. Always wear a hat.
3. Only wear sensible clothes with long sleeves.

What parents do:
1. Rush into the sun and lie stretched out on the deck chair, ignoring all shade and wearing little or no sunscreen. By the end of the first day, they look like lobsters.
2. Refuse/forget to wear their hats —and then drape their heads with towels or (if desperate) handkerchiefs when the heat has burnt their foreheads.
3. Wear as little as possible, which is a

pity, as peeling red skin is not a pretty
sight.

See what I mean? But do parents realize they have
a problem? Will they admit it? Would they believe
it even if we told them? No, of course not—and
why? Because of their completely unfounded and
totally unfair belief in the unwritten rule that:

**Parents Are Always Right
EVEN (or ESPECIALLY)
when they are WRONG**

WELCOME BACK
TO THOSE WHO SKIPPED THAT LAST PART

That is why—to get back to the story (and with
apologies for my little aside)—I was so annoyed. It
didn't matter how much I reminded them of their
previous comments. The more I protested, the
more Mom and Dad backtracked.

It was so perverse. I mean, if I couldn't even rely
on my parents to be the unjust killjoys they
normally were, what was the world coming to?

With these thoughts, and Mom and Dad's relentless, cheery goodwill weighing heavy on my heart, I sank into the deep gloom of the doomed.

Bill, however, remained upbeat and perky.

"No worries!" he said breezily, as he changed into a cod and plopped into the waiting fishbowl. "I've been listening to you and Mom trying to learn the facts on knitting. The only difference between us is that I remember everything and you don't remember anything! Just carry me along to that hall, and I'll whisper the answers to you."

But something told me it was not going to be as easy as all that.

And whatever that something was, it was right.

Chapter 16
THE SCHOOL QUIZ

The school hall was already packed when we arrived. Joe Blagg and his family had kept their promise and done their worst. I was finished. Everywhere I looked, I could see the happy, smiling faces of important-looking guests. Mom was really impressed and kept pointing them out with her number ten knitting needles. There were the members of the press, the managers of local stores and football teams, the school board, visiting principals, the mayor and his wife—even, sitting all alone in a corner, the wretched Donna Mezzweme.

But what really thrilled Mom was that some of my supporters had decided to wear Dad's hideous T-shirts in honor of the event. Had they no taste?

131

In fact, it was all Stacey and I could do to prevent Mom and Dad from rushing home to get some more T-shirts to meet the demand before the tournament started. Everyone seemed in a festive mood;  everyone was having fun; everyone was looking forward to a gripping match.

Except for me.

I was perched on the edge of a chair clutching Bill's bowl to my chest, trying not to panic. My stomach was in knots. My palms were sweaty, and I could feel my hair sticking to the back of my neck. Bill, on the other hand, was as confident as ever. He was splashing about in the water as though he didn't have a care in the world. As for Stacey, she was cramming her face with cake and commenting rudely and audibly on the other contestants. There were about sixteen of them, all milling around the orange juice table trying to act cool. Suddenly, Stacey gasped in dismay.

"Uh-oh, look what the cat dragged in," she hissed. "Princess Perfect and her brother, Einstein. Izzy warned me about them." She sighed and shook her head with frustration. "I thought they were on vacation, but they must have come back early to take part in the competition! Well, bro, I'm afraid to say it, but I think you're through!" And, as if to prove her point, she quickly demolished her third chocolate éclair. Speaking thickly through a mouthful of chocolate and cream, she continued, "Those twins win *everything*. They're the brainiest people on the planet! *She's* at the top of the class at that stuck-up school in the middle of town, and he's at that school for gifted freaky boys on the other side of the road. You haven't got a chance! According to Izzy, Einstein's so bright that he actually knows every single answer in Trivial Pursuit—including the anniversary edition!"

This was all I needed. The Princess was indeed Miss Perfect—gracious, glossy, and well-groomed. Even her white, knee-length socks looked as if they were standing smartly to attention without a single wrinkle. Behind her, flawlessly sorting out a Rubik's cube, walked her tall, geeky-looking twin. One glance at this brainy duo and I knew that we were sunk. And if we weren't going to win, we might as well pack up and go home—why prolong the agony?

Sighing with relief, I was just about to make my move when Stacey gave a second gasp. Struggling for breath, she seized my arm with such a vicelike grip that I almost dropped Bill's bowl.

"*Ow!*" I yelled indignantly, as water splashed onto the floor.

"Ssh!" hissed Stacey. "Be quiet or he'll see you!"

"*Who?* Who will?" said Bill, leaping frantically out of the water. But Stacey wasn't listening. Instead she had jumped up and was squirming around on her tiptoes, 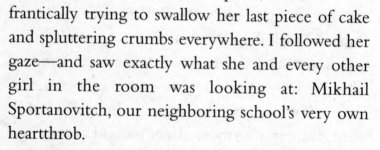 frantically trying to swallow her last piece of cake and spluttering crumbs everywhere. I followed her gaze—and saw exactly what she and every other girl in the room was looking at: Mikhail Sportanovitch, our neighboring school's very own heartthrob.

His fans—every single girl in our school—call him *The Dude*. Bill and I call him *The Dud*. We feel that's a more accurate description.

I groaned. "Oh no, Stacey. Please tell me you're not still crazy about that loser?" I begged. "He's a complete waste of space!"

Stacey was just about to launch a blistering defense of her hero, when Bill decided to stick in his fin's worth too. He considered his sister carefully through the glass and said, "Do you know, Stacey, that you've gone bright pink? It must be all that cake. I wouldn't let him see you like that—pink really clashes with your bright red—"

"If you say *hair*, I will personally feed you to the nearest cat!" spat Stacey.

"All right, Goldilocks! Keep calm! I was actually referring to your pimples!" retorted Bill in a huff.

Stacey lunged furiously at Bill's bowl. Once again, I barely managed to keep a grip on it.

"Will you stop it?" I growled at my siblings. "I'm about to die out there and all you can do is trade cheap personal insults!" Honestly, I thought I was about to have a fit. Luckily, before I did either of them grievous bodily harm, the principal bustled in, looking grim. Judging from his face, he was also having second thoughts about choosing me to represent the school's intellectual elite. Seizing me by the wrist, he insisted on checking my pulse, which was racing.

"Aha!" cried Mr. Peaseby triumphantly. "Just as I thought. The boy is overstressed. No wonder, with

all he's gone through recently. Withdraw, dear boy, withdraw. Let someone else take your place."

He smiled and looked up. He was just about to summon Ike Pearson, the school nerd (special subject: The Ten Best Teachers of Brackenbridge School and How to Spell the One Hundred Longest Words in the Dictionary Backward) to take my seat, when he found himself confronted by Joe Blagg's mother, clutching her nasty-looking handbag.

"What's wrong with the snotty little scamp, then?" she demanded.

The principal shuffled his feet. "He's, um, got a headache—sadly—and is feeling rather faint. I think it might be wise to send him home. I'll just go and get his parents." He tried to inch away from Mrs. Blagg, but only succeeded in bumping into her equally ferocious husband.

"A little off-color, is he?" demanded the car

salesman menacingly, thrusting his shiny red nose into Mr. Peaseby's face. "Maybe I should just give him a little once over, then, just to check that he's all right? Unless," he paused, taking a large wrench out of his pocket and gently tapping it against Mr. Peaseby's arm, "*unless* what you're telling me is a load of old baloney?"

The principal, completely unnerved, threw in the towel.

"No, no, that won't be necessary," he stuttered. "I'm sure he's only suffering from nerves and the heat in the hall." He turned to me and shook my hand.

"Right, Ned," he said, "you'll just have to do the best you can." He looked grimly resigned to an afternoon of failure for the school. "Good luck," he said. "And be careful with that bowl."

I sighed and struggled to my feet. I couldn't blame him for trying to replace me. I only wish he'd succeeded. With legs like lead, I made my way to join the other contestants. Competition volunteers handed each of us a red placard with a large black number on it. Mine was number thirteen. This was no coincidence. The volunteer who gave it to me was Joe. I took one look at his smug smile and almost refused to put it on. But what was the point?

I trudged slowly up the steps to the platform. Three of the other contestants had taken their seats already:

1. The Dude, a.k.a. Mikhail Sportanovitch (special subject: Shot-put Heroes 1923–Present Day)
2. Princess Perfect (special subject: Ironing Boards Through the Ages)
3. Einstein (special subject: The Kinematics of Uniform Circular Motion)

Smiling weakly at my rivals, I sat down and gingerly placed Bill on the table in front of me. Instantly, Joe's hand shot up.

"Sir, sir, excuse me, sir!" demanded the bully. "What's Ned got in that bowl? How do we know he isn't cheating?"

A murmur rippled around the hall; press lights flashed. Mr. Peaseby stood up and laughed genially.

"Now, now, Joe. You know very well that this is Ned's fish, his lucky mascot. We can hardly object to it." I thought for one dreadful moment that he might add, "After all, Ned needs all the help he can get." I knew he was thinking that. But instead, he paused and looked pointedly at the other pupils. "Especially as everyone else has a lucky charm—even Mikhail Sportanovitch!"

It was true. In front of each contestant was something lucky. Einstein had his Rubik's cube (rumor had it that he trained his hands to twist it at spectacular speeds); Miss Perfect was fingering some Greek worry beads, and *The Dud*—or sorry, *Dude*—

was fidgeting with a rather cumbersome rubber ball. He dropped it as soon as his name was mentioned, and it bounced all over the floor and finally fell off the stage. There was an unseemly scramble as a herd of she-elephants (led by Stacey) rushed to retrieve it. Blushing furiously, she finally emerged from the fray disheveled but triumphant and coyly returned the ball to her hero.

I sighed. Bill was right. Stacey's pink face did clash badly with her red pimples. Mikhail languidly pushed his hair back from his eyes before raising the ball above his head like a trophy. There was a gasp of admiration from the girls, followed by a burst of applause.

Joe realized that his complaint had failed. Bill winked at me from the bowl (it seems that fish who have been boys can do this), and blew a few bubbles in mock relief. Then everyone settled down. There was a short silence, and then the tournament began.

At first the questions were easy. Each was drawn at random from a box with hundreds of cards in it. Apparently a group of retired teachers met every Wednesday evening at a bar to think them up. We wrote our answers down in batches of five and handed them to the principal at the end of each round. The contestant with the least correct answers had to leave the platform. I survived the first eleven rounds and saw the expressions on the faces of my friends and family change from sympathy to surprise.

By the twelfth round, there were only a few of us left, and the questions had become much, much harder. Of course, I hadn't a clue what the answers were. I was only there courtesy of Bill, and so far our plan had worked. I would pretend to look very studious when in fact I was staring at Bill's fishy lips. Then, hunched low over my paper, I would scribble down his reply while my ear was glued to the bowl, his tiny voice confirming what I had lip-read. We'd rehearsed our technique for hours, and to begin with, all went well. No one suspected a thing. But then:

1. **Bill started to get bored.**
2. **Joe started to get suspicious.**

It all started when *The Dud* took three minutes to answer question nineteen. It was a math problem. This stumped him. So far, only his encyclopedic knowledge of sports and a big dollop of good luck had carried him through. Now, however, he was dumbstruck. There was a tense silence as *The Dud* rolled his eyes and tried to work out the answer to the question (or, as Bill uncharitably whispered to me—the meaning of the question). As the seconds ticked by, Bill decided to lighten the atmosphere by jumping out of the water a couple of times. Someone in the audience tittered. Encouraged, he did a backflip . . . followed by a wheelie. . . and then a double somersault.

By now, everyone in the room was trying hard not to laugh. Their shoulders were shaking with stifled giggles. Spurred on by the attention, Bill performed a perfect triple somersault. The audience roared with approval, whistling and shouting for more.

The Dud was furious, but eventually he conceded defeat and swaggered off the stage, muttering darkly about a conspiracy. There was a collective groan from his fan club and Stacey looked murderously at me and Bill.

"How *could* you?" she mouthed.

The principal gave me a stern stare and told me to control my bowl. I muttered to Bill to stay still, but he was enjoying himself way too much to stop.

"Okay, okay," he panted. "Keep your scales on. Here's the deal." He did a neat aquatic pirouette before facing me from the fishbowl.

"You have to let me have the top bunk and promise not to poke my butt through the mattress, even if I wriggle about!"

Only my determination to wipe that smug smile off Joe's face kept me from grabbing that cod brother of mine by the gills and . . . I nodded imperceptibly, and Bill swam off gracefully, mission accomplished. Gritting my teeth, but swearing privately to get even with my brother at the first opportunity, I settled down to concentrate on the rest of the tournament.

To be fair, Bill kept the correct answers flowing, and it wasn't long before we were down to the last three contestants:

Princess Perfect
Einstein
and
The Finn Family Duo.

I suddenly had a vision of all that awesome equipment stacked in our living room, and of the look on Joe's face as I was left, the sole winner, on stage.

But we weren't in calm waters yet. Bill began to fool around. He took longer and longer to answer my questions. Instead, he would circle the bowl, stare in the opposite direction, or float on his back blowing bubbles. I glared at him. But power had gone to Bill's scaly head. As part of his so-called "new deal," I was now supposed to not only give him the top bunk, I was also supposed to:

1. Make his bed every morning.
2. Take his turn to unload the dishwasher.
3. Give him 70% of my candy money—and 50% of my allowance.
4. Take his turn to clear out the guinea pig's cage and change the cat litter.

5. Let him have my seat by the window on long car journeys, rather than telling him to sit in the middle because he is the smallest.
   And . . . worst of all . . .
6. Let him have dibs on the PlayStation and the surround-sound cinema system.

What choice did I have? My brother was holding me ransom, and I had no alternative but to give in to his demands. I had just reached the end of my line (a request that I should *always* let him be banker in Monopoly—he cheats every time), when something unexpected happened. Princess Perfect, the Queen of Cool, made a series of mistakes and was forced to leave the tournament.

This was it! Me versus Einstein! Somehow, some way, Bill and I had worked a miracle and reached the final countdown. Brackenbridge School was one step away from winning the Interschool Quiz Championship. Bill and I were one step away from entertainment heaven. And even better, Joe, the school bully, was one step away from his well-deserved comeuppance.

Bill, finally sensing the gravity of the situation, settled down and started to concentrate. The tension was electric. You could have heard a fish sneeze. Mr. Peaseby, sweating slightly and as excited as anyone about the possibility of his school winning the Interschool Quiz Championship for the first time in sixty-three years, stood up to ask the final question.

But Joe Blagg wasn't beaten yet. He realized that if I won this point, then not only was he going to lose all his money, but so were his parents and half the school. He could contain himself no longer. His fat pink fist shot up into the air.

"Sir, sir!" he cried impatiently, charging onto the platform. "It's not fair. Ned is cheating! I know he is!"

There was uproar. Mr. Blagg, who could see his ill-gotten cash disappearing, had to be forcibly restrained by the football coach. Donna Mezzweme began to stamp her stilettos in fury. She had told anyone who would listen that she was ready to order a brand-new sports car, just as soon as this wretched—or rather, wonderful—competition was over. But now that it looked as though she would lose her money *and* be stuck with her useless car, she was not happy. Not happy at all.

Mr. Peaseby, who was as surprised as anybody by my miraculous transformation from class idiot to top brainiac, was furious.

"Cheating! *Cheating?*" he thundered. "And just how, Joe, do you think Ned cheated?"

"With this," yelled Joe. He seized the fishbowl and held it above his head.

The principal blinked. "Not that lucky mascot business again, Joe. You can't seriously expect me to believe that Ned is somehow being told the answers by a *fish*?"

Someone snickered in the audience. Cameras flashed. The journalists, smelling a good story, were scribbling furiously. Mr. and Mrs. Blagg shifted uncomfortably in their chairs.

But Mr. Peaseby hadn't finished. He had been whacked by Mrs. Blagg's handbag, threatened by her husband, and bullied by her son too often not to savor the moment of their downfall. He took a deep breath and stroked his chin thoughtfully.

"Of course, Joe," he continued, "we do know that you and your family have bet a fortune against Ned winning the contest—wasn't it the money for your family vacation? So, obviously, you are very concerned that you are going to lose it." There was a tense silence. "So, this is what we'll do. I'll put the fish here on my desk, where I can keep an eye on it. Ned," he turned to me and pointed, "will sit there at his desk. Dear me," he chuckled gently to himself, "I know that eating fish helps increase brainpower, but I never realized that listening to them could help you win a competition!"

There was a ripple of laughter from the audience, followed by a raucous cheer. Joe, red-faced and furious, stomped back to his seat. I started to sweat. This was the pits. Even Einstein looked uncomfortable.

Mr. Peaseby cleared his throat. "Okay, you two!" he said sternly. "Listen hard! This is the last question of the competition. Ned's special subject. If he answers it correctly, he will win the Interschool Quiz Championship. Are you ready, Ned?"

I think I nodded. I can't remember now. My heart was hammering and there was a pounding noise in my ears. This was it. The final point. If I got this question right, Brackenbridge School would win the cup, and we would get our PlayStation and all the other gizmos. But how could I, when Bill was so far away from me?

There was a deathly hush. I glimpsed Mom from the corner of my eye. She had abandoned her frantic knitting and was clutching Dad's arm as though her life depended on it. Stacey made a thumbs-up sign to me, and I noticed that both she and Izzy had their fingers, legs, and arms crossed.

The principal cleared his throat. "Okay," he said sonorously. I couldn't help feeling like he was enjoying himself a bit too much now. "Here is the last question. I will ask it only once. You will have exactly thirty seconds to make your reply. Think very carefully before you answer." He paused and took a deep breath. "In knitting, what kind of stitch would remind you of . . . " he paused dramatically, "an oyster?"

There was a tense silence. For one ghastly moment, my heart stopped still. I felt clammy and sick, as the all-too-familiar sense of panic welled up in my stomach. The seconds were ticking by: thirty, twenty-nine, twenty-eight, twenty-seven . . . My mind was a complete blank. *What kind of stitch? An oyster?* I stared frantically at Bill, but though he was jumping excitedly up and down out of his bowl, it was no good. I couldn't possibly hear his tiny voice from where I was sitting.

Suddenly, with only fifteen seconds left, the enormity of the situation dawned upon me. I had been cheating, and now I was going to get caught. Joe was going to win. I had lost my chance at revenge and it was all my own fault. How stupid could I get? Looking around the room at the sea of expectant faces, desperately willing me on, I felt nothing but a sinking sense of guilt and shame. How could I ever live this down? I had failed myself, my school, my family, and my friends. The clock was still ticking—ten, nine, eight . . .

I stared numbly around and suddenly caught Mom's eye. And as soon as I saw her—*I remembered!* I couldn't believe it! I, Ned Finn, knew the answer! We were going to win the cup after all!

As the final seconds ticked away, I jumped up and screamed out the right reply: "The purl!"

There was a deafening round of applause. Children

cheered (which was generous, considering so many of them were now broke), teachers clapped each other on the back, and my parents hugged each other with delight. Brackenbridge School had won; Joe Blagg looked like a fool, and the Blaggs and the beastly Donna Mezzweme had lost their money. Life could not get any better. Unless, of course, your name was Ned Finn, in which case you were one of two things: a dead hero or a live coward. Over the applause, I heard the unmistakable screech of the marine life manager's voice:

"I want that fish!" she cried. "Dead or alive! It is MY fish! It came from MY aquarium!"

I had no choice.

I grabbed Bill's bowl and decided to run.

Unfortunately, so did Joe, Thrasher, and Crasher. It was just like old times.

I headed for the boys' locker room. Stacey and I had agreed that it was the best place to turn Bill back into a boy after the tournament. Joe, hot on my heels and an expert in toilet-bullying, pushed me toward the sinks and slammed the door shut with his right foot.

"Okay, you slimy little eel," he snarled, grabbing my collar. "Tell me how you cheated, or I'll flush your fish down the toilet!"

I took a deep breath. Winning was one thing; losing one's brother was quite another. I was about to confess to everything when there was a deafening yell. A stall door burst open behind Joe and out shot Stacey, hurling toilet paper rolls. Thrasher and Crasher, who had just arrived at the scene, were so startled at seeing a girl in the boys' locker room that they tripped over each other and fell to the ground. Joe, equally surprised, let go of my collar. Then, realizing his mistake, he lunged for the fishbowl. But he slipped on some soap and landed in a heap on top of his hapless henchmen.

"Let's go, Ned!" shouted Stacey.

I didn't need to be told twice. Without losing any more time, we rushed out of the locker room, down the hall past startled groups of chatting parents and friends, out of the main door, through the school gates, and straight for home. For the moment, we were safe.

But as I turned the corner onto the main road, I looked back over my shoulder and saw Joe. His fist was punching the air in fury and he was yelling just one word: "*Revenge!*"

Chapter 17
CODNAPPED!

As soon as we reached home, we hid Bill, still in his bowl, in the shade behind a large leafy plant. He was looking a little green after the hurricane we'd created in his fishbowl as we ran home. Leaving Stacey to guard the back door, I raced up to his bedroom to get some bags of Dad's Super-Strong Fish Chips from the box in my wardrobe. Stacey had dropped our supplies when she grabbed all the toilet paper rolls, and we just had to hope that the cleaners would mistake them for the usual snack food wrappers when they cleaned the boys' locker room the following morning.

But when I went into the bedroom, I had a nasty shock. The room had been ransacked. The wardrobe was lying on its side with its door wide open. It was completely empty. The box of Dad's secret fish food was gone. I couldn't find a single packet, however hard I searched. Instead, lying on the floor, I found a business card:

I ran to the window and called down to Stacey. When she came up and saw the devastated bedroom, she sat down on the bottom bunk, put her head in her hands, and began to sob.

"What are we going to do now?" she cried.

I stared at her, speechlessly. But just then, Mom and Dad appeared at the door. They had been running and were out of breath.

"I knew it!" said Dad, snatching the card from my hand. "*DONNA MEZZWEME,* my foot! That woman's a phoney. A crook! An industrial spy! *And* a master of disguise—that's why I didn't recognize her. She's no more a marine life manager than I'm a T-shirt designer. I suddenly realized it when she began screaming at the end of the tournament. Her real name is Madge Sprod. She was once a brilliant scientist, but she's now a notorious con woman who makes her money by stealing other people's ideas and selling them to companies for vast sums of cash. She's always been after my experimental fish foods—even the ones for household pets. She's desperate for anything that will make her rich! And now that I have hit upon a way of saving the world's fish stocks, she wants my formula more than ever! Who knows, she might even be working for that dastardly bunch of crooks, the Underwater Underworld. I've been told they'd stop at nothing to sabotage my attempts to restock the seas with fish!"

Dad sat down on the lower bunk next to Mom. Luckily, he didn't put his head in his hands, as Mom's manically clacking knitting needles would have put his eye out. But I could tell that he was feeling defeated.

"But, Dad," I cried, before I could stop myself, "it's even worse than you think. She's stolen all your new fish food, so now we can't help Bill! He might be a fish for the rest of his life!"

Dad peered at me. "Billy? A fish?"

I had let the cat out of the bag—or rather the fish out of the fishbowl.

Mom abruptly stopped knitting, the needles frozen in mid-stitch. "What do you mean—a fish? What's going on?"

I looked at Stacey. She nodded. It was time to tell all.

First we explained how Bill had become a fish. And then how he hadn't.

Next, we described Joe's jealousy and his challenge to me that I should represent the School in the Interschool Quiz Championship.

After that, we forced ourselves to admit how we had cheated in order to win the contest. (It took quite a lot of squirming and wriggling to confess the truth.)

Finally, I described the fight in the boys' locker room and Joe's threat of revenge.

Mom and Dad listened to us in silence. Then Mom calmly put down her knitting and looked Dad straight in the eye.

"Dan, tell me the truth. Is this possible? Could Billy have eaten your special Super-Strong Fish Chips and turned into a . . . " she had to force herself to say the word, "*cod*?"

Dad stood up and shifted uneasily from foot to

foot, but answered truthfully. "Yes, dear, I'm afraid it could be. You see, when I invented my special formula for restocking the seas, a large company gave us some new chemicals to try out—probably the same company that's now paying Donna-what's-her-name as its spy! Well, the company promised me its stuff was safe and completely harmless. I thought it might improve our formula, so I tried it out. What a mistake! So far, I've only used it in one of our recipes to strengthen the formula—and look what's happened! It's vital that we get our hands on the rest of these bags before anyone else changes shape! We must destroy them all. And I promise, I'll never, ever use an unnatural ingredient again!"

Mom nodded. "Good idea!" she agreed, jumping up off the bed. "Children, I think what you did was wrong, but I know you acted with the best of intentions. What we need to do is to sort out this problem, and fast. First, we must change Bill back into a boy. Luckily, I just happen to have a few extra samples of Dad's special formula fish food in my bag . . . " She delved into her bag of wool and brought out a carrier bag stuffed full of Dad's special Fish Chips. "Don't ask me why, but after

Miss Fish Face's visit, I took some from the wardrobe. I had a hunch that they might come in handy!"

We stared at her, open-mouthed. Mom is brilliant when things are tough. When she's in this kind of mood, nothing can stand in her way. We ran over and gave her a hug.

"Okay," continued Mom decisively. "There's no time to waste! Donna will be on her way to the airport by now with Dad's chips! We need to call the police. Ned, Stacey! You go and feed this food to Billy and change him back into a boy. Dad and I will go to the factory and destroy all the old formula and every single speck of the chemicals.

This must never happen again!"

We nodded enthusiastically and ran downstairs, ready to introduce Mom and Dad to their odd-looking son.

Except we couldn't, because Bill's bowl had disappeared.

All that was left was a badly written note.

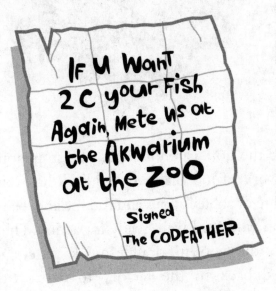

Bill had been codnapped!

Chapter 18
REVENGE OF THE KILLER WHALE

I read the note carefully. It looked suspiciously like the work of Joe Blagg. I could tell his writing—a mixture of abbreviations and bad spelling—anywhere.

Mom and Dad were ready for action. They drove us to the zoo in double-quick time and then rushed back to the factory to destroy the bad formula and any remaining bags of that particular batch of Fish Chips. Our job was to find Bill and to persuade Joe to give him back. Mom—our amazing, dynamic mom—had made herself crystal clear. We were not, under any circumstances, to do anything rash.

It was a pity, therefore, that in our haste to reach the aquarium, we did not notice the broken-down crock of a car by the side of the road. Its one careful lady owner was none other than that crook, Donna Mezzweme. (Madge, to her friends—so I doubt anyone calls her that!) When she saw that we were heading for the zoo, she decided to sneak along and see what we were up to.

It was the end of the day and everyone was going home.

Everyone, that is, except for Joe and his two sidekicks, Crasher and Thrasher.

Joe was holding the fishbowl. As soon as he saw us, he grinned and plunged his hand into the water.

"Look what I've got here," he taunted, pulling Bill out and waving him about by the tail. "It's your disgusting little fish."

Then, dropping Bill back into the bowl, he walked up to us and stuck his thickset jaw right into my face.

"Now look here," he said, with breath that made sardines smell good, "I don't know how you cheated and, quite frankly, I don't care. But I DO know that you cost me a lot of money, and I want it back. So here's how it is:

"One, you tell me how you did it.

"Two, I tell the principal.

"Three, he tells everyone else and gets them to give me my money back.

"Simple, ain't it? Okay then," he said, looking at me grimly. "This is your last chance. 'Fess up or your fish gets it."

And once again he plunged his fat hand into the bowl and hauled out Bill.

I looked at my brother. Bill winked.

"Please, Joe—" I began. But Joe wasn't having any of it. Grunting at his henchmen, he heaved himself onto their shoulders and leaned precariously over the side of the pool, dangling Bill by the tail.

"Kylie!" he called. "Nice fishy! Good killer whale! Come and see what Uncle Joe has got for you . . . a nice, tasty fish finger!"

Stacey nudged me in the back. Kylie was swimming backward and forward, her slim black fin slicing the water like a blade. Bill, however, seemed quite relaxed. I could almost swear that he was talking to Kylie—and then I remembered that, of course, he could! Hadn't Bill told Kylie a joke at their first encounter? I relaxed and looked my brother in the eye.

He winked a second time.

Joe was getting bored.

"Okay, that's it," he said angrily. "I'll count to three. If you haven't told me your scam before I finish, then this floating garbage can can have her smelly snack. Okay . . . " he said. "One . . . two . . . "

And that's when it happened. Joe was just about to count to three, when Kylie's big black nose reared out of the water, right in front of Joe Blagg's face.

"Aaagh!" screamed Crasher and Thrasher, letting go of Joe and running away.

"Aaagh!" screamed Joe, falling into the tank.

"Yippee!" laughed Bill, jumping from the bully's hand and diving into the aquarium. "Isn't this fun!"

"Fun!" I spluttered. "What happens if Kylie eats Joe?" For Kylie was chasing Joe around the pool, snapping at his ankles. But although it looked as though she was going to bite him each time, in the end she only bumped him with her nose.

Bill laughed. "Don't worry. Kylie's only playing with him as revenge for me. I've told her what's been going on. Isn't it lucky that I can speak fish?"

Bill was born lucky. But I was not, and what little luck I had was most definitely about to run out. I quickly fed Bill the two bags of Dad's Super-Strong Fish Chips. With a whizz and a flash and a bang, he turned back into a boy. Then, ignoring my fear of water and going completely against my better instincts, I dived into the tank and rescued the worst bully the school had ever known. Stacey and Bill cheered loudly. With their help, I heaved Joe over the side of the aquarium and back onto dry land. Fat, wet, tired, and thwarted, Joe lay sprawled across the ground, panting for breath. Thrasher and

Crasher were nowhere to be seen. It was time to go home.

But just then, I felt a tap on my shoulder.

"Um, Ned," said a horribly familiar voice that sent shivers down my spine. "It's Donna Mezzweme here. You know, the (former) manager of the aquarium, the (FUTURE) star of Hollywood, and the (presently) broke gambler with a BROKEN-DOWN CAR!" She coughed and regained her composure. Her long, scarlet talons rested on my sleeve. "Well, if you don't mind, I wonder if you could tell me just EXACTLY WHAT IS GOING ON?"

Chapter 19
WINNING THE CATCH

I spun around and stared at her in a panic. If Bill had turned back into a boy in front of Donna Mezzweme, she must have seen everything! What on earth were we going to do?

Luckily, before I could answer, Dad and Mom rushed up.

"Ha! Ms. Donna-Madge-Sprout, or whatever your name is!" snarled Dad, looking most un-Dad-ish. "I see you're up to your rotten tricks again! Well, this time, *this* time, I'm going to call the police!"

"You wouldn't dare!" Donna sneered, peering down at him from over her glasses. "For if you did, *I* would have to tell them all about your fishy food—and," she paused and looked at Bill, "YOUR

EVEN FISHIER SON!"

Mom groaned and clutched Stacey to her chest. I think she was looking for comfort, but since she had a pair of knitting needles sticking out of the top of her jacket pocket, all Stacey felt was a jab in the chin.

The pain seemed to galvanize Stacey into action. It hurts me to say this after all she'd put me through, but I was proud of my sister. She turned and squared up to the former zoo boss.

"Look, Donna Trout!" she said, stepping deliberately on the woman's foot, "I don't know who you are or why you're here, but I *do* know that you are a thief and a crook and that . . . " and she took a deep breath, "I ABSOLUTELY CANNOT STAND YOU!"

And with that she grabbed Donna's hair. Turns out, it was a wig—and a handy place under which to hide some stolen bags of Dad's special fish formula!

"I knew it!" bellowed Dad.

"Stop her!" screeched Mom.

But Donna was too quick for them. She turned and started to beat it down the path, surprisingly fast for somebody wearing six-inch stiletto heels.

Bill, unconcerned as ever by the lengths to which

we had gone to rescue him, had wandered around to the other side of the aquarium for a private chat with Kylie about the bulldozer that was parked there. But when he saw Donna scampering off, he had one of his moments of genius.

"Quick, Dad! Take the bulldozer! The keys are in the ignition!"

Dad didn't need to be told twice. He jumped into the cab and the machine roared to life. Dad gave chase, with everybody, except Joe Blagg, running along behind.

As he caught up with Donna Mezzweme, he lowered the bulldozer's bucket, leaned out the window, and shouted, "You're in a mess, Ms. Mezz. I advise you to give yourself up! Otherwise I am going to scoop you up in this bucket and put you in the water with Kylie." Dad laughed. "And, between you and me, I don't think she's your biggest fan! In fact, I have it on good authority . . . " and he turned and winked at Bill, "that she thinks you're rather dull!"

This was too much for Donna. "*DULL!* ME?" she screeched angrily. She stopped dead in her tracks, swung around—and stumbled into Dad's perfectly poised bucket.

"Ha! Gotcha!" Dad said triumphantly. Raising the bucket into the air, he turned around, drove back to the aquarium, and tipped Ms. Mezzweme straight into the water with Kylie.

Donna was beside herself with rage. But she couldn't protest as Kylie, thrilled to have this chance for revenge, chased her around and around the aquarium, poking Donna's bottom with her nose and forcing her to swim faster and faster. Finally, exhausted and spent, Donna begged for mercy.

"Help me!" she begged, trying to avoid Kylie. "Get me out of here!"

"Only if you say please," said Mom, who's a great stickler for manners.

Donna glowered and ground her teeth. "All right then, help me, *PLEASE!*" she muttered.

"Fair enough," said Mom, taking out a notebook. "We'll get you out of there, but *only* if you promise to do the following things.

"First: you must give back every single packet of Dan's fish food."

Wet and defeated, Donna Mezzweme nodded her head.

"Second: you are going to write to the zoo and say that you have resigned and that Dan is to have your job, as well as supply Kylie with food. I also think you should give some of that money that I can see poking out of your handbag . . . " she pointed to a large canvas bag that Donna had dropped on the ground, "to the zoo so that they can make this horrible aquarium more fun for Kylie! After all, it's not only got to look good, it's got to feel good, too! By the way, you told everyone that you had lost every penny you had betting against Ned—so I can only suppose that you've stolen that money from the zoo!"

Donna glared at Mom and clutched her hands to her chest. "Never!" she spat.

But Mom reached for Stacey's cell phone and started to call the police. Donna knew when she was beaten. She nodded and sniffed.

"Can I get out now?" she asked grumpily.

Mom shook her head, putting the phone away. She still hadn't finished.

"And third," she continued, "you are going to recommend that Joe Blagg is employed here every weekend. After all," she reasoned, "if he's busy here, he won't be able to bully anyone—and he'll be able to earn back all his parents' vacation money that he lost by betting Ned wouldn't win the tournament!

"Then you are going to go to the airport and you are to get on an airplane to anywhere you want to go and you are never, ever going to come back or try, ever again, to steal Dan's fish food or any of his other inventions. Nor are you going to tell anyone what has happened, or I'll make sure that Kylie (or one of her friends) comes and eats you for breakfast. Do I have your word?"

Looking as sour as a pickled herring, Donna Mezzweme agreed to all of Mom's demands. Mom wrote the points down on a piece of paper and Donna signed it—plus a declaration that she had done it of her own free will. Then, and only then, did Dad, Mom, Stacey, Bill, and I haul her out of the water and lead her toward her run-down car.

"Where are you going to go?" I asked her, watching Dad collect all his missing bags of Super-Strong Fish Chips for Scarce Sea Fish and put them with the others by the wall of the aquarium.

Donna, putting on her wig and regaining her confidence by the second, sniffed. "Hollywood!" she announced immediately. "I am fed up with being an industrial spy and sneaking around the place like a thief! From now on, I'm going to give up my life of crime! I have a dream! *I* am destined for better things than this stupid zoo with its pathetic duck pond—I am destined to be a star!" But at that moment she tripped over her bag and broke the heels of her shoes. In her stockinged feet, she looked quite small.

Soon, Donna Mezzweme was gone. We would never see her again. Now all we needed to do was deal with Joe. We found him, damp and surly, but true to form—eating.

Joe had ignored everything that had been going on. Instead, he had been chomping his way through Dad's remaining special Fish Chips. There wasn't a single packet left.

Joe was going to turn into a fish.

And there was nothing we could do to help change him back.

It was not a pleasant sight.

First, Joe went green, then yellow, and then red. Then he blew up like a big balloon. His shoulders rose up to his neck, and his knees dropped down to his ankles.

He had turned into the biggest, ugliest bloater fish the world had ever seen.

"AAGH!" shouted Mom.

"AAGH!" Stacey and I yelled.

"Yippee!" croaked Kylie (or so Bill translated for me later). "A toy!"

And that is almost the end of this fishy tale. Joe dived into the pool and didn't come out for almost three weeks. Soon, he was Kylie's best friend. As he explained later, he had always hated school and any kind of work. He was much happier here, showing off to an audience, safe in the knowledge that he was the biggest and ugliest fish in the world.

Nor did Joe's parents seem to mind—or at least not after Dad had explained everything to them very carefully several times. Once they realized that Joe was only suffering from a temporary condition, they actually looked rather relieved. Removed from their son's evil influence, they decided to give up their life of swindling and open a pooch parlor instead. Together, they groomed the pets of the rich and famous. Their modern and dramatic hairstyles—specialties include "The Afghan Elvis" and the "Punk Rock Poodle"—were photographed worldwide.

And so, it seemed everyone was happy. Dad ran the aquarium, Kylie had a friend, and Bill was a star: the boy who swam with the whale.

And by the time Joe finally turned back into a boy, guess what? He was a changed person (well, almost)—and the school's strongest swimmer. He won all the championships for miles around, and when he wasn't busy ploughing up and down the local swimming pools, he spent the rest of his free time helping to look after the other animals at the zoo. Even if he had wanted to bully anyone, he simply did not have the time.

And as for those terrible T-shirts: you know, we managed to sell every single one, just as Goofy Geoff had predicted. Thanks to the newspaper coverage of the school tournament, Dad managed to sell all the remaining 19,776 of them. They became that season's must-have fashion item—and Dad, with the help of the principal, used some of the profits to pay back everyone (with the exception of Joe Blagg and Donna Mezzweme) who had bet against me. As for Goofy Geoff the printer, he became the most talked-about man in town.

And me? I was pleased. Not only had we managed to save Bill and defeat the local bully, I had actually won the PlayStation, the plasma TV, *and* the surround-sound cinema in the tournament. Mom and Dad were cool about it all and let me keep every single thing—though I had to swap rooms with Stacey again, as they didn't want it in the living room. Stacey didn't mind, though. She was allowed to redecorate her old one in whatever colors she wanted—though why she decided on bright pink and lime green baffles me. So everyone was happy, everything was fine . . . though I must confess a tiny secret . . .

I *still* cannot look at a fish without checking if it really is a fish . . . or just my brother Bill in disguise.

FIN